A River in the Ocean

By Michael Allen

Copyright © 2013. Michael Allen.

All Rights Reserved.

Dedication

This book is dedicated to my daughter who has always been the most incredible person to ever come into my life. Years ago, I experienced a miracle and I had no idea how big it actually was. I just remember thanking God that you had come into the world healthy. Since then, you have always managed to put a smile on my face and warmth in my heart. I love you!

Table of Contents

Chapter I 1

Chapter II 12

Chapter III 23

Chapter IV 32

Chapter V 42

Chapter VI 56

Chapter VII 66

Chapter VIII 76

Chapter IX 86

Chapter X 98

Chapter XI 109

Chapter XII 119

Chapter XIII 128

Chapter XIV 137

Chapter XV 147

Chapter XVI	158
Chapter XVII	169
Chapter XVIII	178
Chapter XIX	187
Chapter XX	195
Chapter XXI	204
Chapter XXII	213
Chapter XXIII	224
Chapter XXIV	235
Chapter XXV	246

Chapter I

They loved the Rappahannock River. It was their favorite place to go. He loved getting her in the water after the wild rapids had calmed down for the year and she loved sitting between his legs when they sat on the bank.

When he was younger, he would hit those same rapids with his friends. They would start at the dam miles up the river and jump off into the pool of water forty feet below. Then, the drift would slowly pull them to the edge of what he affectionately referred to as "Chutes and Ladders."

Two big rocks stood at either side where the top of this adventure started. You could stay there and hold on all you wanted because at that point, the water wasn't strong enough to thrust you through. It was when you let go that you were suddenly in for a ride. All of a sudden, your body twisted and turned around rocks and jetting streams that were perfectly formed by nature itself.

Five miles down the river, the water finally slowed to where you could put your feet down and walk yourself out onto the bank. That's where one friend was always staged to get everybody and drive back up to the dam for another ride.

Throughout his life, Chris Ferlin had always been drawn to Fredericksburg, Virginia, the home of that particular part of the Rappahannock River. His travels often took him to other places. But, he always found a way to come back.

While he was married, he would just pay visits every once in a while. When he got the chance, he would drive hundreds of miles on a weekend to come from Western Maryland to Fredericksburg, Virginia just to spend a day or two where he called home. But, his marriage only lasted a few years until his wife fell ill and finally succumbed to her disease.

Krista was only two years old at the time. She had no idea what death meant. Memories of her mother slowly faded and Chris had no time to mourn either, he was too busy staying on top of Krista's every disaster. If it wasn't a broken video player, it was the cat screaming to get away. How could he mourn with such an energetic little lady running around the house so full of life?

But, one thought did occur to him when he finally got a chance to think for himself. Why was he still living in Western Maryland? Nothing was keeping him there any longer. So, homebound is where his heart was and homebound it would be! Somehow, he knew he just might find happiness again.

It had been two years since they had moved. Krista's old life was fading and new memories in the new town were slowly taking its place. The smallest things were so huge to Krista, and Chris hadn't noticed but his pain was slowly fading as well while investing every ounce of energy into the daughter he loved so dearly.

Today was a special day and for no particular reason. Chris had simply woken up that morning thinking he would pack the day full of great things for Krista and himself to do. They would definitely visit the Rappahannock River, just what they always loved doing together. But, there were other things he had in mind as well.

The first thing would be a trip to the jewelry store where Krista had fallen in love with a locket weeks before.

Chris chose to have it specially engraved with Krista's nickname. With a soft voice of surprise, "Daddy, it's bootiful!"

Chris was kneeling beside Krista, "Yeah? I knew you'd like it. Look at the engraving inside."

"What does it say?"

"That's your nickname."

In a gentle whisper, "It says Kissy?"

"Sure does honey! It says, 'I love you Kissy!'"

"It's like my birfday. Is it?"

"Is it what honey?"

Her little finger explored the locket, still in a whispered tone, "My birfday?"

"No, but it is a special day."

"What day is it?"

"It's just a day I wanted to make special for you."

She suddenly turned to him and gave him a huge hug with a bright smile across her face. Chris picked her up and then nodded to the clerk as they began to leave the store. On their way out, a gentleman was entering and he held the door open for Chris and Krista.

"My dad makes special days out of regular ones."

"He does, does he?"

"Yep! He did it today!"

"Well, that's great!"

Chris smiled at the gentleman and thanked him for holding the door open. The man nodded in return and smiled at Chris with admiration for such a wonderful little girl.

The river was particularly alive. Water splashed high off of the rocks and pulled fallen branches from the bank as the river raced endlessly past their spot high up on the side where the water couldn't reach. Chris and Krista settled in comfortably just above a tree on the northern bank.

As Chris reflected on a day when he and his friends were "body surfing" the Rappahannock, Krista snuggled between his legs and looked out over the water with her father. Then, she looked at her locket and opened it again.

"Kissy," she whispered into the sound of the white water roaring past them.

"Kissy is my favorite," Chris answered.

Krista smiled and put her head back against her father's chest, "Yep."

"Want to watch a movie?"

"Yeah!"

"Which one?"

"That one that has the blue dinosaur."

Chris thought for a second, "You mean a green dragon?"

"Yeah!"

"Ok. We will watch the green dragon movie."

"I like that one."

"I like that one too."

They stared at the water a little longer enjoying a few more moments of the wonderful day they were having. Then Chris stood up, picking Krista up with him. She laughed as he swung her in the air and brought her back down to his arms. She smiled as he looked deep into her eyes and then she wrapped her arms around him as far as they could reach.

"Let's go watch a movie!"

"Ok," she answered with a long, drawn out breath.

Chris turned and started up the path that led to the road where he had parked his car.

After eating dinner and popping in a movie, Chris was well aware that it had been a long day for Krista. Her eyes were heavy when she sat on the couch beside her father. But, she played with her locket and then she looked up at her daddy.

"You like it a lot?" he asked.

Shaking her head, "Mm hm, it's bootiful."

"It's bootiful? You're bootiful!"

Krista smiled and put her head into Chris's arms. She struggled through half the movie and then finally went down for the count. He watched the rest of it by himself as Krista slept gently against him.

But then, he heard the rain slowly start on the window sill. A few drops at a time started to pick up more and more until it was a full blast rain beating against the window. Normally, that's a tranquil sound Chris loves. But, not when he suddenly remembered he left his keys in the car.

Slowly removing himself from the couch, he was careful to keep Krista's head still. He laid her back on the couch and made sure her blanket covered her, she seemed sound asleep. He went to the closet to get his jacket and an umbrella. Then, he walked back over to Krista and stroked her hair.

"It's bootiful," he said. Then, he walked toward the front door and opened the umbrella.

Krista stirred awake enough to watch as her father walked out the door. A dark silhouette with an umbrella over his head was the last she saw of him. She fell back to sleep on the couch, comfortable and warm under her blanket.

Chris's car was parked on the side of the road. The driver's side seat pointed out toward traffic. The rain had picked up and the clouds made everything so dark. Chris was but a silhouette on the side of the road.

He reached into the driver's side door and pulled his keys out of the ignition. Then, he locked the door and shut it behind him. As he turned around, a truck was rounding the corner and lost control.

Running into his car, it sent Chris flying over the hood to land on the sidewalk ten feet away. The truck barreled down the road a few hundred more feet until it finally came to a stop. The driver got out of the truck and ran up the street toward

Chris. As soon as he saw Chris, he started yelling, "Call nine-one-one. Someone, please call nine-one-one."

People inside their homes had heard the crash. A few came out and one responded to make the emergency call. An ambulance arrived shortly and EMTs worked hard to keep Chris stable. They cautiously put him on the stretcher and wheeled him into the back of the ambulance.

The truck driver gave the police as much information as he could. Other police officers talked to a few neighbors about Chris, but no one knew him. The ambulance driver signaled once and then drove off into the dark, rainy night. As the ambulance pulled away, the entire neighborhood was gathered to watch. They shook their heads and talked amongst themselves, not one of them was any the wiser about the little girl sound asleep on the couch in the house just a few feet away.

Chapter II

Krista woke up bright and early. She rubbed her sleepy eyes and looked around at the sunny room, her hair a mess. Throwing the blanket off of her, she planted her bare feet on the hardwood floor.

Running to her room, she went right into her routine. She rooted out a pair of socks and a new outfit. Happily, she changed her clothes and put on her shoes all by herself. Talking herself through it as she did it, Krista remembered all about the rabbit ears her father had taught her. She was excited to show him.

She ran back into the living room and took a seat on the couch, her hair still an awful mess. With her hands on her knees, she waited patiently for her father to come out of his room. But, seconds turned into minutes and minutes seemed to drag on longer and longer. Krista couldn't help herself but to eventually get restless.

She looked up at the door in deep thought. The last thing she remembered seeing was her father leaving through the front door. Maybe, he was on the other side. So, she decided to take an adventure. Walking over to the front door, she looked around the room and back through the kitchen. No one was there. So, she turned to the door and twisted the knob.

The door opened into the outside world. The sun upon her face, she looked around. It was very bright and this was somewhat new to her, she had never before gone this far alone. Down three simple steps she inched her way. She took a seat on the last step and looked down the street.

A huge gap existed where her father's car had been parked. Down the street around the corner, the road just disappeared. It was scary to Krista. But up the street, there were plenty of people that way. It's a marketplace. Krista looked around and her adventurous side took a hold of her again. She stood up and started walking toward the crowd.

She was the littlest person in a huge, lonely world making her way up the sidewalk toward the hustle and bustle of people running in all different directions. They had bags of bread and cups of coffee. They had newspapers and attaché cases. They had beautiful gold watches on their wrists, but no one had the time to notice a small girl in their midst with no one watching her, no one holding her hand.

No one seemed to notice, all but one. In the distance, a lady watched curiously as Krista came into her sight. Maggie was sitting at a café having a cup of coffee and reading a paper. Only the paper was upside down. She hadn't noticed because she was too busy peering out over the top of it.

Whispering to herself, "What in the world is a baby doing walking around by herself?"

She watched as Krista looked around confused. Then, Maggie looked around to see if anyone else was noticing this little girl. After a minute, she decided this had gone on long enough.

Standing up, she walked over to Krista, "Hey honey, whatcha doing?"

Krista put her finger in her mouth and shook her head. The look of worry started to show on her face.

"What is a little thing like you doing out here all by yourself?"

Krista just shook her head. She had no idea what to say.

"Are you hungry?"

Krista nodded.

"Ok, come with me and we'll get you something to eat."

Maggie reached down for Krista who went right up in her arms. Maggie held her close and smiled, "Good girl. We'll just go over here where I was having my coffee and see if your mom comes along okay?"

Krista shook her head, "No mommy."

"No mommy. Are you saying you don't have a mommy?"

Krista just shook her head.

"Where is your dad then?"

Krista's face showed more worry as she shook her head, "I don't know."

"Oh, dear. You don't know? Well, we'll sit over here and wait ok?"

Krista nodded, still with her finger in her mouth. So, Maggie nodded in confirmation and turned on her heels. She walked straight back to her table and got the attention of a server.

When Gilmer arrived in the parking lot a half an hour later, he had no idea what to expect. Maggie stood up and then picked up Krista. Gilmer watched in confusion as Maggie carried the little girl from the café to the truck. Then, she opened the door.

"What in Sam Hill is that?"

"Look what I found. What do you mean what in Sam Hill is that? It's a baby."

"Yeah!"

"I found her."

Gilmer looked at her, "What do you mean you found it?"

"She was walking around by herself. Quit calling her an it!"

"By herself? What in the world?"

"Yeah, she was just standing there. And she let me pick her up."

Gilmer looked around the area where Maggie was pointing. There was no one of distinction who stood out from the busy crowd. Looking back at Krista, "I'm sure she belongs to someone."

"Oh, no. No. I looked."

"You looked?"

"Yeah, I looked around to see if anyone had lost her and no one came."

"Well, what do you want to do?"

"We can't let her walk around. It's going to get dark soon."

"How much you think we can get for her?"

Maggie slapped Gilmer on the shoulder laughingly and then looked down at Krista who was slowly falling asleep in her arms.

Gilmer could see it was a losing battle, "Ok, close the door."

"Really?"

"Yeah, I'm sure she'll be better behaved then your dog was."

"Hey, Jake was a good dog."

"He never ate one of your shoes."

Gilmer started up the truck and put it in reverse. Backing up, he turned to the left until he was in the clear. Pulling forward, he drove the truck to the parking lot exit close to where Maggie had pointed out where she found Krista. Making a left out of the parking lot, he drove down the street, past Krista's home and around the corner to where they disappeared out of sight.

Maggie came down the steps, straight through the living room to the kitchen where dishes were piled up in the sink, "She's down for the count."

"She went down without a fight?"

"I would have to imagine she's pretty tired. Who knows how far she walked before she found me?"

"It's odd."

"What's odd?"

"A kid that age just walking around by herself and nothing on the news."

"Well, you know how this world is getting."

"I can't imagine that though."

"What, that someone could abandon someone so precious?"

"Yeah, that…" Gilmer started walking through the living room.

"Don't you go fidgeting. I just got her down."

"Yeah, woman."

To herself, "Don't yeah me. Mind me."

Standing at the door to the room where Krista was sound asleep, Gilmer looked in on her, a silhouette against the hallway light behind him. He entered the room slowly and walked over to the bed. Sitting softly down beside her, he put one hand on the other side of her.

He stared at her long and hard, thinking deeply about the little girl who now occupied the guest room. She was as peaceful as an angel, breathing softly against her pillow. It wasn't every day the guest room had an occupant, or the house had visitors for that matter.

He reached up and put his hand on the side of her head. Then, he stroked her hair back behind her ears. That's when he saw it. Maybe it could tell him a little more about who she was. He put a finger underneath the chain and followed it slowly to the locket.

Looking closer at it, he was able to snap it open with his finger and his thumb. Small, a little heart with a tiny engraving was hard for him to see at first. He studied harder, "I love you Kissy. Kissy, huh?"

Chapter III

Days, months and years went by while Chris struggled to stay alive in the hospital. There were times when he showed signs he might come out of his coma. But, those signs would fade and he would soon slip ever deeper.

After he had only been in a coma a few months, one nurse in particular took a special interest in his case. It might have been the fact that he had no next of kin and no living will.

It might have been the fact that he had no name and was a complete mystery. But, she would visit on him every day.

She used just about every trick she could think of to stimulate some kind of reaction from him. She held his hand and stroked his arm. She spoke to him without a name, so she called him Steven after a brother she had lost in the war. She seemed to find comfort in calling him by that name.

One day while she was reading to him on her lunch break, his eyes came open. As he moved his hand, it caught her attention out of the corner of her eye and she looked up in wonder. Placing the book on the end table, she stood up and held his hand. She spoke his name and then realized it wasn't really his name. So, she just spoke to him.

It wasn't long before a flood of nurses entered the room and were swarming around him. They were reading his vitals and trying to speak to him. He just looked straight out into the world with his eyes wide open. He didn't respond to anything anyone was saying and he didn't move his stare. Then just as soon as he had come awake, he slipped right back into his coma.

A few years went by before another episode occurred. By this time, the nurse who read to him had eventually found a way to move on from her own painful memories of her brother and moved on from sitting by the side of Chris. It was a much younger nurse who came in to check on him one day and found him staring straight at her.

Like a ghost staring into your soul, his eyes were dead inside but locked on hers. She was scared stiff. Her eyes grew wide as she dropped the clipboard. Then finally finding her legs, she ran out of the room screaming.

Once again, nurses rushed into his room and swarmed around him. They tried to get his attention by waving their hands in front of his glare. But, his eyes didn't move a bit. They grabbed his hands, but his hands didn't grab back. It wasn't long before his eyes grew heavy and he fell back into his lonely sleep.

In total, nine years went by while Chris slept peacefully in a hospital bed. He was being kept alive with machines that monitored his brain activity and drips that slowly kept him fed throughout the day. Nurses looked in on him every once in a while, but they mainly kept track of him at their desk where computers displayed everything they needed to know.

That is until one day while a nurse was handling several tasks at once, she happened to notice a change in Chris's vitals. She didn't think anything of it at first and finished her other tasks. But, soon came back to check the computer again. This time, she knew there was something happening.

She immediately went to Chris's room and as she entered, his eyes looked straight at her. They followed her around the room as she walked over to the monitor and read the output. She looked at him and started speaking softly.

"Can you hear me?"

Chris's response was sluggish, but he looked at her and moved his eye lids. That was enough to let her know that he was awake and aware. Again, a team of nurses soon rushed the room. But this time, it was not a drill. He was awake and he would stay that way.

"Mom," Krista yelled as she ran down the steps.

"What dear," Maggie hollered back from the kitchen where she was doing dishes at the sink.

"What is dad doing," Krista asked as she walked to the kitchen door and looked through the window.

"Oh he's doing what he does honey," Maggie answered as she dried a plate and looked out the window herself. She squinted to see the barn in the distance across the yard.

Krista had her hand on the door knob, but she hesitated to open it. Maggie looked over at her with a slight smile, and then looked back through the window with concern.

"Yeah, I don't know if I'd go out there either dear," Maggie said as she dried her hands. "You never know if it's safe."

"I mean, how dangerous can it possibly be," Krista asked. "He's just looking through a telescope. It's not like he's blowing stuff up or burning anything to the ground."

"Well, go on then if you want to see what he's doing."

"Too late! Here he comes."

Krista stood back from the door and waited patiently for Gilmer. It took him a few seconds, but soon he was barreling through the door in a rush.

"What in the world are you doing Gil," Maggie asked as soon as Gilmer entered the kitchen.

"I'm trying to see if I can find the Sombrero Galaxy," Gilmer shot back.

"The what now," Maggie asked.

Gilmer stopped and looked at Maggie for a second, "I was watching a show this morning that was talking about the Sombrero Galaxy. It was named that way because of the hat, you know the one the Mexican's wear."

"And why is it so important to you," Maggie wondered.

"Because they said it was really expensive. I don't get it. I mean, I haven't been able to find it yet. I think I'll have to wait until tonight to see if I can get a better look. But, why is it so expensive," Gilmer asked.

"Dad, because it's really big," Krista answered.

"But, that's the part I don't get. Why in the world are we paying for it," Gilmer asked.

Maggie and Krista looked at each other with concern. Maggie shook her head while Krista furled her eyebrows. Then, they both looked at each other again.

Maggie started, "What uh, what?"

"I mean, how much is this thing costing us and why is it even up to us," Gilmer answered with his own questions as he looked at Maggie and then at Krista. "I don't even understand what we're paying for."

Krista studied hard on Gilmer until all of a sudden, something dawned on her, "No dad, it's expansive."

"Yeah, that's what I'm saying," Gilmer interrupted. "But, what in the world is all that money going on?"

Holding her hands in a circle and then gesturing outward, Krista tried to make sense of it, "It's expansive."

"Yeah, I know," Gilmer added. "But, why can't the Russians or even the Chinese, for crying out loud, help us pay for this thing?"

"Wow dad," Krista put her hands on her hips and shook her head. She started to explain again, but Maggie's expression told her that it was no use. So, she just gave into it. "Ok dad, let's take a look at it later on tonight and see why it's so expansive."

"I might have to get a bigger telescope or rig that one so that we can see further."

Maggie instantly warned, "Don't rig it up too much! Don't need you burning your eyes with strong lenses, like, you know, how a magnifying glass burns an ant."

"Mag, I know what I'm doing. They're only going to be pointed out way."

Krista looked back and forth between Maggie and Gilmer as they discussed the impossible feat of turning a store bought telescope into a high powered astronomical observer. Somewhere in the back of her mind, she knew that the conversation was all wrong. But, she couldn't figure out who was more wrong.

Chapter IV

It was clear Chris was frustrated. He had been working all morning on trying to remember his name. With his head resting back against his pillow and his eyes staring at the ceiling, he shook his head and tried to form sounds with his mouth.

Janet had been assigned his case when the Department of Social Services was notified that Chris might need help assimilating back into life. So, she visited him as often as she could to figure out what resources he might have if any, and what she would have to do for him if he needed anything. But, it had to start with figuring out his name.

"Come on! You can do it. Try to remember anything and it might come back to you," Janet urged.

Chris looked out the window and stared at a tree blowing in the wind. He soon found himself swaying with it and trying to think of the last time he had seen a tree before his coma. He looked at the television in front of him and tried to think if he could make a connection there. Then, he looked at Janet.

He stared at Janet for a rather long time and then a thought crossed his mind. He put his head back against his pillow again and tried to form the sounds with his mouth, "...F. Ferl. Ferlin."

"Ferlin?"

"K. Kri. Kris…"

"Ferlin, Chris. Uh, ok. That sounds like a name. Chris Ferlin might be your name. You know what? Relax. Try to remember anything else that you can. But, let me look into this and then I'll come back later today after I run this name, Ok?"

Chris nodded his head. He had a look of some relief on his face. He wasn't quite full of excitement. But at least, they were further than they were the day before. Hopefully, the fact that he came up with a name might get them somewhere.

"Hey, we'll get through this. But this is something. You might be Chris. It will get easier. But for now, you just might be Chris ok?"

"Ok."

On the front porch, Maggie was rocking in her rocking chair enjoying a glass of sweet tea and watching Krista read while she sat comfortably in the sun on the first step of the porch. Gilmer was on the other side of the porch with his glass of tea. He was staring intently at Krista until he decided to speak what was on his mind.

"I should teach you how to protect yourself Kissy."

Krista looked up from her book, "Huh, what's that?"

"Yeah, you know? There are all sorts of people out there and some of them aren't up to any good. I should teach you how to protect yourself from them," Gilmer answered.

"Oh, for crying out loud Gil. Can't you find something better to do? After all, I got her doing her schooling," Maggie interrupted.

"Oh, is that what she's doing? You already started her on that," Gilmer asked.

"I told you last week, I was going to start her on schooling," Maggie answered.

"So, she already started on that. Well, this will only take a second," Gilmer urged.

"I said go find something else to do. Don't you have something to do," Maggie asked.

"No, not really," Gilmer answered.

"Well, what have you been doing," Maggie asked.

"What do you mean? I had a good week. I already sold fourteen cartoon woodpeckers and two cases of shine. Plus, I have a free truckload of corn coming because Jarod's wife wants a bent over lady," Gilmer answered.

"A bent over lady," Krista asked.

"Yeah, ladies love them," Gilmer answered. "It looks like a lady bent over in the yard like she's picking up something. But, you're looking straight at her butt."

"Oh yeah, I've seen those," Krista said. "You make those too?"

"Every once in a while, someone will want one," Gilmer answered. "Anyhow, come on! Let me teach you one move to protect yourself when you're in town."

"Oh, this oughta be good," Maggie remarked as she looked at Gilmer and shook her head.

Krista put her book aside and then stood up as she stepped up to the porch. Gilmer gestured for her to come to him, "Now, turn around."

Krista turned around and Gilmer started giving her instructions, "Sometimes, a guy will come up behind you and grab you like this." Gilmer wrapped his arms around her. "What I want you to do is, first cross your legs."

Krista crossed one leg over the other.

"That's good," Gilmer praised. "Now, take this hand and punch straight back with it." Gilmer pointed at the hand he wanted her to use.

Krista thought about it and then punched as hard as she could. Staring straight forward, proud of her ability to follow his instructions, she asked, "Like that daddy?"

The look on his face showed remarkable pain. Maggie could hardly hold her composure. Squeaking and forcing between broken breaths, he finally answered, "Yes, honey. That was good!"

Maggie covered her mouth with her hand. Krista jumped up and down as she clapped. Maggie shook her head, "Ok, I think we're done with the karate lesson for today. Come on back and read your book some more honey."

"Ok, mommy."

Gilmer bent over and then found his way back to where he was sitting. After straightening up, he crossed his legs and took a drink of his tea. Maggie was still holding back her laughter.

Krista looked up at Gilmer, "Are you sure that was good?"

Still with broken breath, Gilmer answered, "Yep. That was very good honey."

Chris was watching the television as Janet entered the room. She appeared to be in good spirits bringing Chris some great news. Chris couldn't help but get excited as he turned the volume down on the television and gave Janet his undivided attention.

"You look like you have some good news to tell me," Chris observed.

"I do. I really do," Janet answered as she stared at him with a huge smile on her face.

"Ok, you're killing me here," Chris said.

"Ok, here it is. That is your name. I know I was supposed to be back to tell you this the other day. But, I got wrapped up in business concerning your name and what else I have to tell you."

"Oh yeah," Chris asked.

"Yeah, so you're Chris Ferlin. Aren't you excited," Janet asked.

"Well, I am. But, I kind of knew that. I mean, it just felt right once it came out of my mouth," Chris answered.

"Oh, good. You're already used to it," Janet said, and then she took a seat. "Well, it appears that you have a bank account and an insurance policy. So, you have money. A good bit of it I might add."

"Well, that's one less thing to worry about," Chris remarked.

"Yeah, that's what took me so long to get back to you," Janet continued. "The insurance company was trying not to pay because they said the policy had lapsed. But, I made sure they understood that it was active when you went into the coma. It was fully paid at that time. So, the insurance company has to pay the bills on your stay here, which I've been able to negotiate down quite a bit. I mean, taking into consideration the circumstances. But, they also owe you a considerable income on your insurance policy."

"Oh man, that's great news," Chris said relieved.

"I thought you'd like that," Janet said.

Silence filled the room, but the tone was rather heavy. Chris was very relieved. Walking away from a situation like this is very overwhelming. He lost nine years and he has no memory. But, it would be worse if he had no resources either.

Janet understood the gravity of her news and let the awkward silence linger a bit longer, "So, when they are ready to release you from here, you don't have anything to worry about. You'll have enough money to get back on your feet and start getting back into your old life."

Chris stared at Janet for a second, taking in the meaning of the last words she had just spoken. It wasn't exactly going to be that easy. What was his old life? He couldn't remember the last thing he had done. He had no idea what he used to do or even where he used to live. In fact, it wasn't going to be easy at all.

Chapter V

Krista sat at the kitchen table waiting patiently for Gilmer. Maggie was staring back at her and then her thoughts started to drift back to when they first found the little girl. She started to recall the memory of how she figured out how old Krista actually was.

Every year as they had done since the day they found her, Maggie and Gilmer had thrown a birthday party for Krista. On the day that they found her, Maggie marked it special on the calendar and couldn't wait until exactly a year had passed to celebrate the new addition to her home.

By the time Krista had turned five, Maggie had divined a way to figure out her true age. Well, that's what she told Gilmer anyway.

"Kissy will be turning five this year and I want to throw a special birthday party for her," Maggie told Gilmer.

"How do you know she turns five," Gilmer asked very curiously.

"You have to be smart. I got her to tell me," Maggie pointed to her temple as she winked at Gilmer.

"Oh," Gilmer responded with a drawn out sigh that he was very impressed.

In all actuality, it didn't quite go down that way. Maggie had been in the kitchen looking through her catalogs marking down all the wishes she dreamed about, knowing full well that she would either get a second-hand version of what she wanted or Gilmer would try to make it for her. That was her life and she was used to it although, a new washer and dryer would be nice. Even a new coffee maker would put a smile on her face.

As she sat at the kitchen table dreaming about new things, Krista found her, "What you doing?"

"Oh, I'm just dreaming about things I'd like to have," Maggie answered.

"I do that," Krista said with a bright smile.

Maggie's eyes opened wide, "You do?"

"Yeah," Krista said excitedly. "I tell daddy and he gets it for me. He got dis for my birfday."

"He did," Maggie asked. She was curious about the man and where he might be. But, Maggie didn't want to pursue it. She thought if he wanted his daughter so bad, he should look for her. And she had found nothing in the news or posted anywhere around town about it. So, she kept it to herself. That's how she had decided to handle it. For now, Krista was in good hands and she would cross that bridge when she came to it.

Krista started, "Well, it's not my birfday. My birfday is a whole nother day. He just do it. He just got it. I'm four and it has my nickname. I'm Kissy."

Maggie didn't push for Krista's real name either. She was happy calling her Kissy and that's the way that was going to be. At least, now Maggie knew how old she was and that was the start of the birthday tradition.

Krista was thirteen this year. She waited patiently while staring at the cake in the middle of the table, "What did dad get me?"

"It's nice," Maggie said as she snapped out of recalling old memories and looked back at Krista. "But, don't get your hopes up. It's not a gun like the one he got you when you were six."

"Oh yeah," Krista soon remembered. "What was he thinking?"

Maggie started laughing as she shook her head. Krista started laughing too as they recalled her birthday just seven years ago.

Maggie knew Gilmer had bought the gun. But, she had no idea it was for Krista. When Gilmer walked Krista out to the barn, Maggie thought nothing of it. She just went about her work in the kitchen and let them have their fun.

All of a sudden, Maggie heard a gunshot. It startled her so much that she dropped a dish on the floor. Looking out the kitchen window, Maggie saw the little girl holding the pistol while Gilmer was kneeling behind her.

The next thing Gilmer saw was Maggie storming off the back porch with a broom in her hand. She practically flew across the yard how fast she was moving. Gilmer couldn't think of anything else to do, but to run to the other side of the barn and get as far away from Maggie as he could.

Meanwhile, the six year old princess was holding a pistol and in all the excitement, she turned toward Maggie to see what all the fuss was about. Maggie stopped dead in her tracks. She dropped the broom as she put her hands out to caution Krista, "Don't pull the trigger," she said in slow, paced words.

"Hi mommy," Krista smiled. "Daddy teached me."

"I know," Maggie said trying to keep herself from getting overly excited. "Let me see it."

"Ok," Krista said as she started walking the gun toward Maggie.

"Stop," Maggie shouted, suddenly thinking that if Krista would fall, she could shoot herself. Maggie's eyes grew even wider than they were before. She walked faster toward Krista until she finally was able to step to her side. Then, Maggie reached over Krista's shoulders and grasped the gun cautiously. She took it from Krista without an incident.

Straightening up with the gun in her hand, Maggie looked around the yard, "Now, where is that boy?"

Krista looked at the other side of the barn and pointed.

"I felt like shooting him with it that day," Maggie told Krista.

"You wouldn't have shot daddy," Krista said.

"Honey, I was going to shoot him in the foot and teach him a lesson," Maggie and Krista laughed. "But, I couldn't find him anywhere for the longest time. He took off and knew not to even try me until I had a chance to calm down."

Maggie and Krista were laughing hysterically as Gilmer entered the room, "What are you guys talking about?"

"Don't you even worry about it," Maggie answered Gilmer. "Krista is waiting patiently for her present."

"And cake daddy," Krista added.

"Ok, ok," Gilmer raised his hands. "It's actually been under your nose the whole time."

Krista looked up at Maggie, who smiled with a twinkle in her eye. Krista started to look around the kitchen until a bright smile came across her face.

Gilmer knew what she was eyeing, "Warmer."

"No way," Krista said. "You got them?"

"Yep," Gilmer answered.

On the counter, hidden between the napkins in the napkin holder was an envelope that Krista could now clearly see. "You got the tickets?"

"Yes," Gilmer answered again. "But, take a look at them."

Krista jumped out of her chair and ran over to the counter where she immediately grabbed the envelope and opened it. She took out the tickets and screamed when she saw what was also in it, "All day?"

"Yes ma'am," Gilmer said with a laugh.

"We're going to ride rides all day and then go," Krista paused to catch her breath.

"That girl you like," Gilmer laughed.

"To the concert," Krista continued. "I'm so excited. I'm so excited. When? When are we going?"

"Next weekend," Maggie answered.

Krista stared for a second, and then she suddenly screamed. Maggie and Gilmer laughed as Krista gave them both a hug.

Chris and Janet stood in front of a rundown farmhouse. Janet looked at Chris not even half impressed, "It needs some work. But, it's what you asked for I think."

"It's perfect. It will definitely do," Chris answered.

"Really," Janet asked.

Since Chris had awoken, Janet had gone above and beyond the call of duty. It might have been that she looked at him as a helpless creature who seemed new to the world. He certainly wasn't new. But with the brain damage he had suffered, even ever so slightly, there were things he definitely needed help doing in order to be able to move on with his life.

She had secured the funds that were due him and she had taken care of his medical bills with it, also negotiating the entire bill down quite a bit so that he could afford it and walk away with as much money as possible. She was surprised to find out how much the doctors and the hospital in general were willing to write-off so that the final bill was affordable.

Now, Janet had taken it upon herself to find him a place to live. When Janet and Chris had talked about it, he felt he just wanted to live somewhere on the outskirts of town so that his life would be slow and easy. Life in town seemed too overwhelming and something he needed to slowly merge himself into over time. Janet completely agreed and began her search.

What she found was a farmhouse owned by an elderly lady who had moved in town with her daughter years ago. The farmhouse had been on the market, but with no takers. As the farmhouse aged, it was getting harder and harder to sell. Janet wasn't very happy with it. But, Chris could see all the potential in the world.

The house came somewhat furnished and in his mind, Chris thought it only needed a little work. He actually looked forward to getting started as he figured out what he could do for the rest of his life. It didn't take long for it to come to him.

While walking through the house on the first day he owned it, Chris found furniture that needed refinished or were in some state of needing repair. A trip to town in his old weathered truck he bought for nearly nothing, he picked up a few supplies and immediately went to work on the furniture.

The more trips he made to town for supplies, the more he got to know the store owners. One day, someone mentioned needing a piece of furniture repaired and Chris was in business. The store owners referred Chris, and they kept referring Chris. Work started slow. But, word of mouth is the best advertising. Within a few months, Chris was doing regular work and he didn't mind at all.

But, there was something nagging at him. He had a picture in his mind and he couldn't shake it. It nagged at him so much that it often woke him up in the middle of the night and it made him slip into a daydream in the middle of the day. So, he decided to do something about it.

The next trip he made into town, Chris bought a canvas and some paint supplies. On his front porch, he built himself an easel into the banister. He hung the canvas and opened his paint. Then, he grabbed his brush and stared at the canvas for a few minutes.

From the moment he started painting to the moment he was done, he didn't stop working on the canvas. Going from color to color, he painted like a madman. Not able to pull himself away except for the occasional cup of coffee, Chris painted into the evening, overnight and through to the morning hours.

He finally stopped painting and shook his head. Taking a drink of his coffee, he studied the canvas as he took a step back to get a different perspective. One good thought crossed his mind and that was that he found a new interest he loved. He loved to paint.

But, the disturbing thought that crossed his mind was who was in the painting. She haunted him, even though he felt a sense of comfort now that she was on the canvas. He felt so close to her, yet she was just a painting. He couldn't imagine anywhere he had ever met her. He couldn't remember any reason why he even knew her. But, she completed a part of him he had no idea how to describe.

"Who are you," Chris whispered. "It's bootiful!"

Chapter VI

Chris kept painting. Over the next couple of months, he couldn't get the little girl out of his head. So, he kept painting her.

In one painting, she appears to be around the age of five. In her robe, she is standing on a stool at the stove with a spatula in her hand. Her bare feet are lifting her up so that she can see the pancakes in the skillet.

As Chris was painting every detail of this portrait that burned so brightly in his mind, his imagination grew deeper and deeper until the moment seemed to come to life. She looked at him from the stove and started to giggle with five year old playfulness.

"Can I flip them daddy," She asked.

"Not yet honey. You have to wait until the bubbles. Remember," Chris answered.

"But, look daddy," she pointed with her small finger. "There are bubbles."

With a giggle, he looked in the skillet, "That isn't enough honey. Have a little patience."

She looked back at the skillet and with that, the moment faded. Chris stood on his porch for several minutes before he started painting again. The moment felt so real. But, his kitchen was empty. His painting was of something he had only imagined.

His heart sunk. But, he didn't understand why he felt an urging sense of loneliness. It wasn't as if he knew the girl. He was only imagining her. So, there was no reason for him to feel a sense of loss.

Chris started to find another passion as he painted paintings and repaired broken furniture. Soon, he was designing and building furniture of his own. People still brought him broken furniture. But, word started getting around in town that he was also building it and they were requesting pieces when they came out to pick up their repaired furniture.

Pouring his heart and soul into a new chair design or a new table certainly kept him busy. But then, every once in a while a new image would haunt him again. This time, it was of a little girl the age of eight hiding underneath her blanket.

She was sitting up in the middle of the bed so that the blanket formed a teepee around her. He was painting her as she was peeking out from under the blanket. The sound of a giggle made her come to life.

"Find me daddy," she whispered.

"I'm trying honey. Are you under the chair," Chris asked.

The little girl's giggle gave her away as her eyes followed Chris around the room.

"Are you in the desk drawer," Chris asked. "No, you're not there." Chris walked to the other side of the room, "Are you behind the curtain." Chris opened the curtain quickly. "Hmm, you're not there either."

The little girl giggled underneath the blanket and then, suddenly her laughing eyes froze as the shadow cast over her face softened into the painting. Chris stared at her for minutes, his eyes locked on her face until he was able to break his thoughts free. Why does his heart feel so low after these episodes that seem so real?

With a deep sense of loss, Chris turned his thoughts back to his next order of furniture. He began looking at his plans again, and then he carried them with him as he climbed down the steps to the basement where he kept his wood and his power saws.

Looking through his supplies and taking different measurements, Chris's mind never left his thoughts of the little girl who haunted his paintings. He paused for a moment to look out of the basement window. It was a bright and beautiful day, but it had mysteriously become grey to him.

"Daddy, why don't you love me," the little girl asked jerking Chris completely out of his trance.

He had been daydreaming for quite some time. His coffee was cold and his painting was only half complete. But, his imagination was now running wild again.

He could see her riding the bike in the front driveway. She was riding in a circle, up to the mailbox and then back around to him.

He thought he heard her correctly. But, he had to make sure, "What's that honey?"

"Why don't you love me, Daddy," she said playfully.

"Well for one, you're too short. And you're a girl. So, you have those two things going against you right off the bat," Chris answered.

Since he had started seeing visions of her, he had painted many paintings. She was either climbing a tree or running up the road. But, he had also developed a witty and loving relationship with her.

She was always asking him off-the-wall questions, to which he had to learn how to respond. It soon became their common way of joking with each other. She would ask the question and he would have to find a way to make her laugh.

So, he stood up and watched her ride a few more turns in the driveway. Then, he returned to his painting where the girl on the bike was once again frozen in time. It was that moment he hated the most. That was when she had to leave him and he was once again alone, with his thoughts, and his paintings.

The rest of his life was easy to manage. He repaired furniture and he built beautiful pieces. He lived his life on his own pace. He wasn't rushed. He didn't have to be rushed. So, there was nothing in his life that bothered him, except when she came to visit him.

He knew she wasn't real. He was able to keep track of that reality. But, she sure seemed real when she visited. She seemed so real that he truly missed her when she had to leave. It was like a part of his life was missing, and he had no idea what to do about it. He couldn't stop her from visiting and he didn't want to stop her.

But then one day, it just happened. It had been a year since Chris had awoken from his coma. He had painted the little girl in every age from about the time she looked five up until she appeared to be fourteen.

He was sitting on the couch, staring out of the window in front of him as the sun was setting beyond the field in the distance. That's when he noticed her dancing.

In the middle of his living room, she was dancing so lively and singing right along with it. But, there wasn't any music. As he watched her dance, suddenly he could start to hear the music himself.

She twirled and swayed, and then she twirled the other way. She knew all the words and she sung them just like she wrote them. In fact, Chris was quite sure he had never heard that song before. But interestingly, he knew the words as well.

When you miss me,
I miss you too.

Close your eyes and I am there.

When you miss me,

You know what I do?

In my mind, I can see you.

They sang the song together as she danced with a soft glow of light behind her and a touch of wind blowing through the breezeway. As the song ended, Chris rose to his feet and walked onto the front porch where he began painting a picture of the dancing girl.

But, she was gone again. He didn't realize that she was gone until he was finished the painting. That's when the thought occurred to him that he had painted this painting from beginning to end, from evening to early morning, without a break, and without a deep thought of her interrupting his flow.

So, he signed and dated the painting. Then, he put it with the rest of them, in a room where he had hung them all. A very deep, sense of sorrow came over him. It was as if he was putting her away.

He felt as if she had left, only this time not to return. He didn't know why he felt that way, other than there was something different. He had enjoyed her visits for nearly every week now and he had gotten to know her. He knew a certain way about her that was telling him now, something had changed.

Chapter VII

The truck turned the corner and slid, almost hitting a tree and going into a ditch. Rocks and dust flew as the truck accelerated down the back road. The gears were grinding like a blacksmith sharpening a sword.

Smoke billowed out of the exhaust as the truck spat and sputtered up the dirt path that led over the mountain away from town. The back end fishtailed as potholes made the truck catch air and bounce around all over the road. Sliding again, the truck took a sudden turn and shot into a driveway as it pelted rocks across the road and into the fence on the other side.

Coming to a screeching halt, the truck slid about five feet before finally coming to a full stop. Maggie flew off the porch madder than a tiger protecting her cub.

Climbing out of the truck, Gilmer yelled, "Whoa! That was one wild ride!"

"And it's going to be your last if I get a hold of you," Maggie sternly warned as she rounded the truck to catch Gilmer on the passenger side.

"Mom, I have to learn," Krista said as she climbed down from the driver's seat.

"You are fourteen! You don't need to know how to drive," Maggie answered.

With his hands raised like he was getting arrested, "Now Mag, she asked to drive home and she'll be driving soon enough."

"If she asked you for a bomb, would you give her one," Maggie fired back.

Gilmer thought about it for a second and Maggie's eyes lit with fire, "You better never give her any bombs!"

Gilmer raised his eyebrows as he shot Krista a look across the truck bed. Krista's eyes grew wide as she shook her head. Gilmer shook his head back at Krista to confirm that he would keep their little secret.

But, Maggie wasn't stupid. She picked up on the little gestures, "You've given her a bomb before haven't you?"

"No!"

"Gil!"

"We made one," Krista volunteered.

"You what," Maggie yelled.

"It was a small one Mag," Gilmer answered. "We made it in a soda bottle with just a little bit of bleach and transmission fluid is all."

"That's all," Maggie mocked.

"I was right there," Gilmer assured.

"Oh, you were there," Maggie yelled. "So, what? You can blow yourself up for all I care! But if you go blowing her up, that will be the end of you. You'll be asking the devil for first class tickets to hell just to keep me from getting a hold of you. You hear me?"

"Well, yes ma'am," Gilmer answered as he exchanged a look with Krista.

Maggie snapped her head around and stared straight into Krista's eyes.

"Yes ma'am," Krista didn't know why she was answering. But, Maggie's look made her feel as if she needed to say something.

"Ok then," Maggie calmed down and eyed the both of them.

Looking at Krista, Gilmer reminded, "At least she forgot about you driving."

Maggie shot a look back at Gilmer as if a light bulb suddenly came on above her head.

"Wow, dad," Krista commented. "We were almost in the clear."

Chris had just set the legs on a new chair he was making. He left the glue to dry while all the parts were held together with clamps. But, he was on a particularly active schedule this one morning. He went straight back to focusing on his painting.

Sitting on his easel was a painting of a building. He loved capturing the detail of architecture and working with different shading. His paintings ranged from mountain scenes to country settings. He had just recently started to explore different buildings in town. Capturing the way things actually looked on canvas was quite a challenge, but it had become a very enjoyable hobby from which Chris often could not pull himself away.

In the distance, Chris noticed a car coming down his road. Soon enough, it turned into his driveway. Taking an awfully long time, finally a beautiful female emerged from the car. She refreshed her hair and began walking toward him.

Chris had picked up his cup of coffee by this time. It had taken awhile, but eventually Chris got used to having strange visitors during the day. She strolled up to his porch and using her hand to shade her eyes, she looked at him for a moment.

"Are you Chris, Chris Ferlin," She asked.

"Yes ma'am, yes I am," Chris answered.

"Can I see some of your paintings," She asked.

Chris shrugged his shoulders. Then, he lifted his coffee and took another drink.

"Oh, I'm Amy Zamaglias. I own an art studio downtown. I mainly sell art supplies and I even teach some art courses. But, I was told you are a very good painter and I wanted to see some of your paintings. I had a thought that we could talk about selling them at my store."

With his cup in his hand, Chris's eyes grew very wide. Then, his face registered deep thought. "Well, you can take a look at this painting right here and if you think it has potential, I can show you some more I have hanging all throughout the house and stacked up in the garage."

With a large, beautiful smile, Amy answered, "Sounds great!"

She walked up the steps onto the porch and took a look at the painting. Chris watched as she admired it. He felt the urge to say something. But then, he thought he would just let her express her own thoughts about it.

She looked over at him and then back at the picture, "I love how you bring it to life. The finished parts I mean. They seem so real."

"Well, that's what I'm doing with that one," Chris said.

"But, I do abstracts too. That's what I call them. I might paint a building in an abstract way. To me it's a building. To someone else, I don't know what they see."

Amy looked at Chris, "Yeah, that's the fun of art. You can make it whatever you want it to be. And it's great hearing what other people think about it."

"Mm hmm," was all Chris had to say. He had his moments when he had much to say, and then other times he could sum up everything he was thinking in a word or two. In this case, Amy had said everything he intended to say about art.

"Can I see some more," Amy asked.

"Uh, sure," Chris answered. Then, he gestured for Amy to follow him.

Amy took her time. She admired each and every painting like she was inspecting diamonds at a jewelry store.

She commented on some of the pieces. But mainly, she just took each painting in like viewing it was breathing air.

She finally did confirm that she would like to sell the paintings out of her store. Of course, Chris had no problem with that at all. He wondered if they would even sell. But, it made him excited to find out if other people liked them as much as he did.

Amy shook hands with Chris as she carried a few paintings off the porch. Chris followed behind her with a few more.

"I'll be back to get the rest later when I get the truck. But, these will do just fine. I'll make sure to call you when they sell," Amy reassured.

"You sound awfully sure about these selling," Chris remarked.

"Oh, they'll sell! I know people who were already asking," Amy mentioned.

"You do," Chris found this new finding rather remarkable. "Well then, by all means. Sell away."

Amy smiled. Then, she got in her car and drove away. Chris simply shook his head as he watched Amy's car head out of the driveway and up the road. Once again, his life had taken an unexpected turn. What had just happened had the potential of being a great thing. He had nothing in the world to complain about and yet, his life still didn't sit right with him.

Chapter VIII

It's a strange phenomenon in art and it's one that can be debated by anyone with half an opinion. But, some art can be ingenious, inspired, thought provoking and yet go absolutely nowhere. No one feels it when they look at it and no one sees the value in it.

But, the right person comes along at the right time and captures a movement. There isn't any rule to what people will like. It can have a great deal to do with what is going on in the world at that time. It could simply be about the mood, the temperament art enthusiasts might share in a given era.

What happened to Chris was a perfectly orchestrated journey, nothing short of miraculous. One day in Amy's store, an elderly lady bought a piece of his art. The lady's niece was a real estate agent for an upscale condominium unit in Baltimore. The elderly lady gave her niece the painting and it was hung in the model unit that gets shown to potential buyers.

It immediately became a trend when one of the condominium owners purchased his own painting from Amy. It wasn't long before Amy was shipping pieces to half the owners in the condominium unit. And then, the miracle took extraordinary wings when a particular celebrity's aide from Los Angeles was visiting an old friend from Baltimore. When he returned to Los Angeles with one of Chris's pieces, Amy soon found herself selling off every last painting.

Chris's work was suddenly in demand. It was highly requested and many celebrities were willing to pay top dollar to be put at the top of the list. Chris could not believe what had happened. Every star in the universe had perfectly aligned itself to give Chris this opportunity and Amy called every week to see if there were any more pieces for her to sell.

Ironically, the art wasn't hard for Chris to produce. He had a rhythm. He found inspiration from everything he saw. Once he began a painting, it was mere hours before he was finished. But, Chris was slowing down and he loved to design furniture. So, Amy would make a trip out to Chris's house every week and pick up three or four more paintings. Then, she would discuss with him the demand for more.

Chris would help Amy carry the paintings to her car and then watch her drive away. Just before leaving, she always asked for more as if the need would never die and Chris would always promise that he was moving as fast as he could. But, there was one thing he kept to himself.

He walked up to his porch and went inside his house. Then, he went to his special room where he kept a certain collection of paintings. The little girl hadn't visited him in some time. But, those paintings were precious to him. He wasn't about to let them go. Chris would keep painting as long as Amy found a need for his work, but his little girl would never be sold.

Chris continued to make furniture and paint paintings over the next couple of months. It was as if his life was in slow motion. He didn't mind the pace, even though once in a while he would feel as if something was out of place.

The feeling that something in his life wasn't right lingered in the back of his mind all the time. Sometimes, it was but a whisper he could hardly hear. Other times, it was more evident, nagging at him while he went about his day.

It was on one of those particularly lonely days when the world around him felt darkest, that he noticed a different sort of light coming from the kitchen. As he landed at the bottom of the steps, he turned and what he saw filled his soul. She had come to visit again.

"You know it's my birthday Dad," his girl reminded him from the bar in the kitchen.

"Oh, I know," he answered, immediately remembering what it felt like to have her around. He had missed her so much, but he couldn't just call his little angel into existence. She had to come on her own.

"So, what did you get me," she asked excited.

"Actually, I can't wait to give it to you," Chris answered.

"Give it to me now," she cheered as she jumped up and down in the kitchen clapping.

"Ok, ok," Chris laughed. "Follow me upstairs then…Angel," Chris made a mental note that he had finally given her a name. But, it fit her so well. It's exactly how he felt about her. Even though his life seemed lost and empty, she came when he needed her. If there wasn't already a definition for angel, that would be it.

Angel ran across the floor and slid to the stairs. Then, she followed Chris as he took his time. "Come on Dad, you're killing me," Angel said playfully.

"I...am going as fast as I can," Chris answered.

"My birthday will be over by then," Angel remarked.

Chris laughed as he topped the stairs. A small hallway led to four doors. In the space between them there stood a structure with a blanket draped over it.

"What is it," Angel asked.

"Ok, here we go," Chris walked over to the structure. Then in one swift motion, he pulled off the blanket, "Tada!"

There stood a dollhouse, made by the hands of Chris himself. Angel's eyes lit up at the sight of it. She walked over to it and slid her hand across the roof. Then, she followed the workmanship down to the porch. She was fascinated by every detail.

It had everything from actual opening windows to light features she could turn on and off with small switches. Little furniture was in every room. She was so amazed, she even tried the kitchen sink. Chris chuckled softly to himself.

"Well," Angel said. "It has everything else. Had to check."

"So, do you like it," Chris asked.

"I love it," Angel answered softly. "But, it's funny."

"What is," Chris wondered.

"I'm fourteen," Angel answered.

Chris nodded his head.

Angel continued, "Dollhouses are for little girls."

"Well, you are a little girl. You're a little girl to me," Chris protested.

Angel looked up at him, "Dad, I will cherish it! But, it's something a four year old would love."

Angel's words resonated as Chris stood there staring at her. He stared at her for quite some time while she played with the dollhouse. He listened to her hum while she moved furniture and became more fascinated by every new detail she discovered. Then, her humming grew into words.

> We have our memories.
>
> Try to remember me.
>
> Close your eyes and I'll be there.
>
> Think about me
>
> And I will think about you.
>
> In our minds we'll be together.
>
> The times we spend apart
>
> We'll be together.
>
> That's all you have to do when you miss me.

Her voice lingered in the air as the last line echoed throughout the house. Chris found himself looking at a lonely dollhouse. Angel had come and gone. But, she left him with a song. Sung like a nursery rhyme, its meaning was very healing.

Chris stared at the dollhouse shaking his head. For the life of him, he couldn't remember building it. He kneeled in front of it and inspected it himself. To his astonishment, it was very masterful. He admired how much detail he had put into it.

It was strange. But, stranger things had happened to him. He was learning to take everything in stride. So, he moved the dollhouse to one of the vacant rooms and he called the room Angel's. Looking back, the lonely dollhouse sitting in the middle of the empty room was an accurate omen for how he felt, but with an interesting twist of also feeling at peace. She had come to visit, and that's exactly what he needed for the day.

He started down the steps with a beat in his walk. He actually started to think through the rest of his day with purpose and determination. When he reached the bottom of his steps, he started toward the front door on his way to enjoy the porch. That's when he saw her out of the corner of his eye.

In the middle of his secret room, on an easel, there was a painting of Angel enjoying her dollhouse. Chris looked up the steps and recalled the lines she sung. He could hear her singing.

> We have our memories.
>
> Try to remember me.
>
> Close your eyes and I'll be there.

Then, Chris looked back at the painting. It was in exact detail, the dollhouse he didn't remember building, Angel admiring it, everything. That's when the thought suddenly occurred to him.

"Now, when did I paint that?"

Chapter IX

Maggie was rocking in her chair on the porch while she sewed away with her needles and yarn. Krista was lying on her back at the steps of the porch. The day was sunny with a nice breeze, too beautiful to waste cooped up inside.

It was then that the phone started ringing. But, Maggie looked at the phone and refused to answer it. Krista sat up and started staring at Maggie as the phone kept ringing. Maggie simply stared back at Krista with a look that said she didn't care. Krista just shook her head until she finally had enough.

"Are you going to answer that," she asked. "It's driving me nuts," she added.

Maggie cocked her head, "Oh, alright. But, I know exactly who it is!

"Hello, can I help you? ... Now, who is this? ... What's your name? ... And what are you calling about? ... Well now, hold on! I'll try to see if Maggie's home."

Maggie placed the phone down on the arm of the chair and went back to sewing, "Damn telemarketers!"

Krista looked at Maggie with a smile on her face. Then suddenly, she busted out laughing. Maggie tried to hold her expression. But, she couldn't hold it for very long. Maggie laughed right along with her.

They laughed until the phone started blasting the off-hook alert, "They hung up! They hung up on you!" Krista was nearly in tears.

The more Krista laughed, the more Maggie laughed. The two roared in laughter until Gilmer came out the front door onto the porch, "What are you guys going on about?"

Krista pointed at Maggie and tried to explain, "She, she answered the phone. They hung up. They hung up on her."

Watching Krista try to tell the story made Maggie laugh more. Confused, Gilmer had no idea why getting hung up on was funny all of a sudden.

"Who hung up," Gilmer asked.

"Tele, tele," Krista couldn't finish what she was trying to say.

Maggie controlled herself long enough, "Telemarketers."

"Telemarketers hung up on you," Gilmer asked.

Krista and Maggie both nodded their heads while they continued laughing.

Gilmer stared at the girls for a moment until a lone thought crept across his mind. "Well, they must not've wanted the sale that bad," Gilmer observed.

Maggie and Krista both stopped laughing and gave Gilmer the most serious stare they each could muster. It only lasted about a second, and then they exploded into laughter even harder than before.

If it was one thing that Maggie ensured, and that would be that Krista was well-educated. She did her research at the public library and brought home what she thought was the best in homeschooling materials. Krista learned her three "Rs," but Maggie also included history and a bit of science. Krista actually received a much better education than most kids who were getting a public education.

But often, it was despite Maggie's most thoughtful attempts rather than because of them. As Krista sat at the dining room table studying hard in her physics book and drawing diagrams on paper, Maggie took a special interest in what Krista was studying. She sat down fascinated, "What are you looking at?"

Krista looked up, "Um, this is about trajectory and projectile motion."

Maggie's head was resting in her hand as she nodded, but the blank stare told it all. Krista continued, "Well, from what I'm reading and trying to figure out is they seem to be the same thing. A projectile that is dropped goes in motion, so that would be the projectile motion. But, if it were, let's say, fired out of a rifle, that would be trajectory, and still projectile motion. I think anyway."

Maggie smiled and shook her head. But, her eyes were still blank.

Krista continued, "Ok like, if I were to drop a rock from the top of the roof, it would fall at a certain rate to the ground. I could calculate that."

"Oh yeah," Maggie finally pieced it together. "Gravity would pull the rock down to the ground and it would hit at a certain speed. But let's say that we dropped, oh I don't know, the truck from the roof, it would come down faster."

Krista cocked her head, "No. Uh, no, not what I just learned. They would both hit the ground at the same time."

"What," Maggie shook her head. "No way! The truck would hit the ground faster. It's bigger. It weighs more. It would definitely come down faster."

Krista hesitated, "But, the book says that gravity acts on all objects the same. It pulls them to the ground at the same rate."

"No, no, no dear. That's not what it means honey," Maggie argued. "It means that gravity acts on them the same, that it will pull all things down to the ground. But, not at the same speed. That's not possible."

Krista stared at Maggie for a moment. Then, she started rifling through the book. She knew she had just read that part and that she had a good understanding of gravity. The book was logical in that way. Each lesson built on the last. Each portion of physics was dependent on the prior lesson.

"Well, I'm going to go get dinner on the table. I'm glad I stopped in to see what you were doing though. I'd hate for you to learn the wrong thing and then go on thinking that," Maggie concluded.

Krista watched as Maggie walked away. She shook her head, quite sure that she was right. When Krista found that section in the book again, she studied it as hard as she could. She went over the mathematical problems again and again until she knew that she was right.

Krista went over it with herself in a whisper, "The time it takes an object to hit the ground is the square root of two times the distance divided by gravity. Then in that equation, weight is not a factor. I knew I was right."

She never told Maggie. When Maggie brought it up again, Krista just agreed with her. She knew in the back of her mind the way physics actually worked. There was no need to correct her mom about it.

Chris's spirits had been lifted for a few days. But slowly, those feelings faded and Chris went back to feeling like he was a ghost in his own home. He merely moved around in it. His days worked like clockwork with very little deviation.

He rose in the mornings and mapped out his day looking over orders for furniture and thinking about what he might want to paint next. Then he simply moved through the rest of his day, one echoing footstep after another echoing footstep. He really didn't pay that much attention to how he sounded as he meandered around the house. It was just hard to ignore in those moments when his soul was feeling its darkest.

When he was working on his furniture designs though was when he forgot about everything. His high-back chairs were everyone's favorite. But, his benches and what he affectionately liked to call his Unique Series were very popular as well. His benches could comfortably sit two adults, and people most commonly loved putting them in their yards.

But his Unique Series was where he had most of his fun. He loved creating designs no one else could even imagine. Utilizing an actual tree stump, Chris once made a chair that made you feel like you were sitting in a tree. The lady who bought it placed the chair beside the tree in her yard, and then she called them "Big Daddy" and "Little Brother." Chris found the names very flattering. That was the first time he ever heard of his furniture being named. Several more tree stumps soon arrived at Chris's house and he started calling them "Little Brothers."

Another design he loved was when he masterfully bent several very long boards to build the chair with no legs. Seven Eight-foot boards were bent with steam, rope and time to form the foundation, curved back to provide the seat and then turned to extend upward for the back. He even twisted them at the top for extra design. The only dowels and screws that were used were to bind the seven boards together.

The design he was working on at the time was what he called the "Twisted Chair." Each board making up the chair was positioned in a different direction. But sure enough, in the center was a seat and there were arm rests. Chris had to really think this design through to make it work.

As he was studying his work and thinking about what he had to do next, he noticed that his humming had turned into words.

I want to know where do the angels go.

I want know who hides the sun.

"Whoa," Chris thought. "Where did that come from? That's pretty deep. I want to know where do the angels go? I want to know who hides the sun? What does that even mean?"

Chris continued calculating his chair. He made measurements and marked the wood. Then, he picked out a precut plank and started to fix it in place. Before he knew it, he was singing again.

I want to know who keeps watch of you
All through the night.
Angel! Tell the angels you have come.
Tell them I already have one!

As he finished attaching the plank, "Tell the angels you have come? Tell them I already have one?" He nodded his head. It was good. But, where did these new words come from and where were they going?

Chapter X

Gilmer sat silently at the kitchen table with the look of deep worry in his eyes. His hands were clenched tightly in his lap. Once in a while, he would scratch his head or find something to fiddle with for a moment. But, he mainly sat still with his hands clenched tightly in his lap.

When Maggie came down the steps, Gilmer's eyes grew wide and he straightened up his back. Maggie walked to the kitchen nervously drying her hands with her hand towel. She looked straight at Gilmer, but she didn't have any words. Her eyes told the story of someone who was in deep sorrow, and had no idea what to do about it.

"Well, how is she," Gilmer asked.

"Not good! Not good at all," Maggie answered.

"Well, what could it be," Gilmer asked.

"I don't know. She's running a fever. Her temperature is sky high. I've changed her sheets twice, she's sweating so much. It's hard to tell Gil."

"But, she'll be alright," Gilmer looked at Maggie with concern.

"We'll have to wait until the fever breaks. I'll keep her cool with ice until then," Maggie comforted. "In the meantime, run into town and grab some aspirin. Actually, I need a list of things. Here, let me write them down for you."

Maggie grabbed a piece of paper and started writing down items like she was making out a grocery list. She would pause and look up or look out the window. Then, she would continue to jot down a few more items.

Gilmer paced the floor with his hands in his pockets. Once in a while, he would stop and stare at Maggie. Then, he would look at the ceiling as if trying to see through it and look at Krista struggling in her bed. After a moment, he would stop and continue to pace the floor again.

"Ok Gil, here it is," Maggie announced. "Make sure you get everything on that list. Don't leave anything out! I need everything on that list."

Gilmer grabbed the list and looked it over before starting toward the door, "I'll be right back."

"Don't rush yourself Gil. I want you to come back with everything on that list."

"Alright woman," Gilmer snapped back. "I get it. You want everything on this here list. I'll be right back."

Maggie stopped in the middle of the living room floor and looked at Gilmer. Gilmer knew not to look back at her. He just opened the door and slinked his way onto the porch.

Krista's sweaty hair was matted to her head. Staring at the ceiling, she would slip in and out of consciousness. She would be awake one moment, and then her eyes would grow heavy and slowly shut.

An hour or two would go by until she woke up in pain, burning hot and delirious. Maggie treated the fever with ice cold washcloths on her forehead. She pumped aspirin in the poor girl regularly throughout the day. She got Krista to eat some soup every time she could.

But, it was when Krista would wake up with the cold sweats that Maggie really worried. Maggie just knew deep down in her soul that going from hot to cold could not be good. But, Maggie's knowledge of home healthcare was as extensive as getting rid of poison and what to do with a bee sting.

In the kitchen, Gilmer was pacing the floor again. Maggie was at the sink looking like she was about ready to pull all of her hair out of her head.

"What are we going to do," Gilmer asked.

"We have to wait until her fever breaks Gil," Maggie answered. "I've told you this already."

"It has been a few days Mag," Gilmer looked straight at Maggie. "That's why I'm asking again."

"I know," Maggie said. "I'm worried too."

"Why can't we just take her to the hospital," Gilmer asked.

"Because we'll lose her, you know that," Maggie answered.

"Well, we might lose her anyway," Gilmer shot back at Maggie.

Gilmer's words lingered heavy in the air. He didn't intend to hurt Maggie. But, he was concerned and he felt helpless. Let alone how he felt for the poor helpless girl who didn't look like she was going to make it.

Maggie's eyes grew red, and then tears started to stream down her cheeks. She put her face in her hands and started sobbing pitifully. Gilmer couldn't stand when Maggie cried. He felt even worse because the words that had slipped out of his mouth were what made her cry this time.

Through this ordeal, Maggie had kept it together. She was doing everything she thought to do right. But, nothing seemed to be working. Thinking about all this, Gilmer took his hands out of his pockets and walked slowly over to Maggie.

He put his arms around her and pulled her to him. Maggie tucked her face in Gilmer's chest and just let it all out of her system. She cried for minutes. It gave her strength to move on and go attend to Krista again.

She pulled away from Gilmer and looked up into his eyes. Then, she patted him on the chest, "Thank you."

Gilmer nodded his head. Then, Maggie kissed his lips and walked away. Gilmer watched as Maggie left the kitchen. In the back of his mind, he was hoping Maggie would figure it all out and Krista would get well. But, he also had his doubts. This was a job for a doctor, and that was one thing he definitely knew.

Chris was sitting at his kitchen bar with a pen and a piece of paper. He had to admit, he had never written a poem before in his life. But, these words coming into his head were actually alive. He had never felt so strongly about anything in his life.

It wasn't just a thought that had occurred to him. It wasn't merely a stream of consciousness that he could tap into or grasp. The words that were burning in his brain were like a living breathing thing he had to let run like a trapped animal being returned to the wild.

He had written down the words that had come to him earlier. But, he knew there were more. It was as if an empty poem was lying on the edge of his tongue like a breath he couldn't take or a thought he couldn't imagine.

I want to know where do the angels go.

I want to know who hides the sun.

I want to know who keeps watch of you

All through the night.

Angel! Tell the angels you have come.

Tell them I already have one!

There were lines that had been scribbled out and then repeated. Then, they were scribbled out again. But, Chris wasn't frustrated yet. He had just started to write another line when Amy came in the front door.

I remember. I remember you!

Chris looked up from what he was doing and saw Amy walk in the door. She had become quite comfortable just walking in without knocking. Chris himself had become quite used to it as well.

"Well Chris," Amy called as she trotted across the living room floor, "What do you have for me today?"

"I have two paintings," Chris answered.

"Two," Amy asked. "You only have two?"

"I'm sorry Amy," Chris responded, "But, I have been distracted by a stupid poem."

"You're doing poetry now," Amy asked. "You paint and build furniture. Now, you're a poet. Well, color me impressed."

"No, I'm not a poet," Chris answered. "I just have this one poem stuck in my head and I can't get it out. I have no idea where this is coming from."

"Well, let me see," Amy asked.

"It is far from finished," Chris answered. "I just got started."

"Let me see what you got," Amy pushed.

Chris looked at her and then looked down at the poem, "Alright I guess. Here it is. I'll go get your paintings while you're reading what little I have."

"Yay," Amy clapped as she pulled the piece of paper over to herself.

When Chris returned with the paintings, Amy was tapping on the poem with the pen. She looked up at him with concern in her eyes.

"What do you think," Chris asked.

"Well, here's the thing," Amy gathered her thoughts, "You didn't write this."

"What do you mean," Chris asked.

"I've read this before," Amy answered.

"Oh, thank you," Chris said relieved.

"Really," Amy was surprised.

"Oh hell yeah, really," Chris answered. "I couldn't figure out where this was coming from. Now, all I have to do is read it and that will be that. Which one is it?"

"Oh wow," Amy said. "You asked me too quick. I tell you what, I'll try to find it for you."

"Great," Chris was truly relieved. "Now life can get back to normal, whatever that is."

"And that's good news," Amy added. "Maybe I can get three or even four paintings next week?"

"Absolutely!"

Chapter XI

Krista had been mumbling for quite some time. But, it was indiscernible to Maggie what she was even saying. There were very few audible words and in the frequency that they came, it was impossible to put them together and make anything out of it.

Maggie kept refreshing the icy cold washcloth and stroking Krista's sweaty hair. Krista would look at Maggie from time to time, but there was nothing in her eyes. There was no sign of recognition. There was no sign of any comprehension at all. Krista was slipping away and Maggie couldn't do anything about it.

"Is a man," Krista mumbled.

Maggie simply nodded her head and agreed. She had no way of knowing what Krista meant.

"The man," Krista repeated.

"Yeah, the man honey," Maggie comforted.

"Yahs, is umbrella," Krista added.

"Mm hmm," Maggie agreed.

"Hees umbrella, is a man," Krista looked into Maggie's eyes.

"Yeah baby, I know," Maggie comforted. "I'm here honey. I'll take care of you."

"He's there. He's uh, he's," Krista shook her head. She was getting frustrated.

"Now dear, don't get upset," Maggie tried to calm Krista down. "It's alright. I'm here."

"No, mm mum, mm," Krista shook her head again. "The man...he's umbrella." Krista was really struggling to say something. But, it was painful for Maggie to watch.

"Ok dear," Maggie comforted. "Calm down now. I'm here honey. I'm here."

Chris could hear someone calling his name. Then, he realized it was Amy. He looked to the ceiling of the basement and waited again to be sure. But, it was definitely her.

Chris put everything down and walked across the basement to see what was so important. "Coming," Chris yelled as he walked up the steps.

"Oh, there you are," Amy answered.

"Um, yeah, I was just working on my furniture," Chris mentioned.

"Well, I won't keep you long. I just stopped by to bring you something," Amy said as she patiently waited for Chris to reach the top of the stairs.

As Chris finally turned the corner to come into the living room where Amy was standing, "Oh yeah, what did you bring me?"

Amy turned and looked at Chris, "Oh, is that where your basement is?"

"Yeah, where did you think it was," Chris asked.

"Um, I didn't. I never thought about it," Amy answered. "Uh anyway, I brought you the poem."

"Oh, you found it," Chris said with surprise.

"Yeah, I was up all night because I couldn't get it off my mind," Amy said.

"You're kidding," Chris remarked. "You didn't have to do all that!"

"Actually, I did," Amy responded. "I wouldn't be able to get any sleep, ever. Anyway, here it is." Amy handed Chris an envelope.

Chris grabbed the envelope and opened it. He pulled out a piece of paper and began reading.

In Memory of an Angel

I remember. I remember you!

On a warm day…
On the porch swing in the sunlight.
With your flowers…
Singing church songs in your white dress.
I was standing by you when you fell down
And took your last breath.
You were not so old then…
They played the violin over your coffin.

Chris looked up from the piece of paper, "What a morbid poem!"

"Yeah, it is," Amy agreed. "It's about a little girl who died when she was young. Apparently, the guy who wrote the poem knew her and wrote it to honor her."

"Well, why would that be stuck in my head," Chris asked. Then, he looked down at the piece of paper and began reading again.

>Angel! I want to know where do the angels go.
>
>I want to know who hides the sun.
>
>I want to know who keeps watch of you
>
>All through the night.
>
>Angel! Tell the angels you have come.
>
>Tell them I already have one!

A River in the Ocean

A hundred years ago...I've grown a few since

Then.

A thousand miles...a million people I have met.

And yet I still come home to find the place

Where you were laid.

In all my travels...

It's not any easier to get through the day.

I want to know where do the angels go.

I want to know who hides the sun.

I want to know who keeps watch of you

All through the night.

Angel! Tell the angels you have come.

Tell them I already have one!

I was just a kid.

How could you have mattered so much?

You know what they say about angels...

It only takes one touch...

I want to know where do the angels go.

I want to know who hides the sun.

I want to know who keeps watch of you

All through the night.

Angel! Tell the angels you have come.

Tell them I already have one!

As Chris read the poem, he experienced a flush of strange thoughts. The faint vision of a lady faded in and out of his mind. She was sitting in a garden. Then, she was throwing rocks into a stream and laughing.

His face grew hot, and his heart grew heavy. But, it didn't make sense. Chris didn't know the lady in his thoughts. He was sure he had never seen her. But, that's how his imagination worked. Something that wasn't there could feel so real to him.

Chris looked up at Amy. She could tell the poem had a deep and meaningful effect. But, she didn't pry. She only wanted to know what Chris was willing to tell her, and in his time.

Chris couldn't find all the words. But as he looked at Amy, he started to find a few, "It's like I have this whole other life I know nothing about. I'm trying to piece it together. But, nothing is coming. Maybe this is something trying to get out, trying to tell me something. But, I just can't seem to figure it out yet."

"I understand," Amy said.

"Do you," Chris asked. He looked deep in her eyes, "I don't know if I do. I don't know if I understand any of this."

"Well, I guess I don't know what you're going through, uh Chris," Amy answered. "But, I do know this is tough for you and that it's not easy to have to pick up with your life knowing that the first part of it, before your time in the hospital, was a whole other life you know nothing about."

Chris looked at her and nodded.

"We'll figure it out," Amy assured him. She put her hand on his arm, "We'll do it together. We'll try to figure it out! Ok?"

Chris studied Amy hard, "Ok."

Chapter XII

Angel! Tell the angels you have Come.

Tell them I already have one.

Krista opened her eyes and stared at the ceiling. She took in a deep breath and then she looked around the room. Wiping her forehead, she pushed herself up on one elbow and then tasted the dry cotton in her mouth.

"Mom," Krista yelled with a raspy voice. "Mom!"

Maggie was in the kitchen making chicken and using the broth to make soup. She wasn't thinking when she answered Krista, "Yeah honey."

Maggie heard Krista yell again, "Yeah honey!"

Then, Maggie looked up suddenly and cocked her head. When she heard Krista the third time, Maggie dropped everything she was doing and ran up the steps. There, to Maggie's surprise was a half-drained little girl who brought tears to Maggie's eyes.

"Oh, thank God," Maggie said as she ran into the room to comfort Krista. "I'm so happy. Thank God. Thank God. Thank God."

"Mom," Krista whispered.

"Yes dear," Maggie answered.

"Can I have something to drink," Krista asked.

"Oh, absolutely," Maggie answered holding Krista as close to her as she could. "I'll be right back dear."

"Ok," Krista said.

Chris sat at his kitchen bar staring out the dining room window, a cup of coffee between his hands and the poem off to the side of him. He had been studying it all day. Every time he read it, he had another vision of the lady who had come into his thoughts since the first time he read the poem.

He could see her dancing in the living room, but it was a different living room. There were books on the shelf and a wooden lamp. But, that's all he could get before the vision of her faded again.

As he started to read more of it, he could see her hanging clothes on the line. Sheets were blowing in the wind. The laundry was in a wicker basket right by her feet. In his vision, she looked straight at him and laughed. That's when that vision ended.

These thoughts kept circling in his brain. But one thing that brought him a sense of peace was how closely she resembled his Angel. She was older and clearly not the same girl. But, they looked so much like each other.

"I'm finally feeling better today daddy," Angel announced.

Snapping out of his trance, Chris looked over at Angel standing in the middle of the living room. He nodded as a smile crept across his face, "You do? That's great! Come here. Let me feel your head."

Angel walked over to the kitchen area and sat down at the bar. Chris reached across and put the back of his hand on her forehead. Her eyes looked tired. But, she felt fine.

"Yep, the fever broke."

"Told you," Angel said as she looked into Chris's eyes. "You know that poem you have been reading?"

"Yeah," Chris answered.

"It's mom's," Angel announced.

"Mom's," Chris asked. "It's mom's?"

"Yeah," Angel answered. "She loved it. You used to read it to her."

"I did?"

"Yeah, you read it to her," Angel confirmed. "She liked when you did that!"

"Hmm," Chris thought about Angel's words.

He was imagining an entire life. He had a daughter and a wife. But, Angel didn't stick around long enough to tell him what happened to his wife, her mother. As Chris went back to staring out the dining room window, Angel stood up and walked away. Her footsteps faded as she started up the steps.

Chris heard the last footstep echo as he turned to look at the stairs. He grabbed his cup of coffee and walked to his secret room. When he looked inside, the painting of Angel playing with her dollhouse was still on the easel. It caught him somewhat by surprise. But, Chris shrugged his shoulders and closed the door behind him on his way out to the front porch.

That's when he felt the strongest urge to paint her. An image entered his mind, but there was something different about it. That's why he felt so strongly about painting it immediately. It was nothing like any of the other ones.

They were full of life and color. All the paintings he had painted of her were smiling, playful portraits. She was pointing at a bird in a tree or staring out over a river. She was always happy with a sparkle in her eye. But not this painting, it was different.

He painted soft yellow over the white background. Chris always covered every inch of his canvas with paint, even if the background was the same color as the canvas itself. The yellow strokes were wide with gaps, looking like a scribble a child would make.

Then, he started mixing colors and painting her face. But, it was merely lines and shading. Her eyes were sad as they looked down toward the ground. Her hair fell across her forehead and flowed down where it rested on her shoulders. Her chin was resting on her knee and her arms were wrapped around her lone leg.

It was an abstract, with no life and very little expression. The words in the poem suddenly came to mind. But, it wasn't right. Angel was alive. She got better. Her fever had broken and she was feeling fine.

Krista was sitting up in bed eating her soup. She was working on her third bowl since she hadn't been able to really eat for several days. Maggie had tried to give her soup every day, several times. But, Krista couldn't really get any of it down.

As Krista ate, Maggie looked on feeling very guilty and helpless. She was relieved that Krista had recovered from her fever. But she knew deep down inside that she had nothing to do with keeping Krista healthy. If anything, she put the poor girl's life in danger. It scared her how close to death Krista had come.

She placed the bowl on the nightstand and looked up at Maggie. She tried to smile, but she was exhausted. Maggie nodded her head and smiled back, understanding fully that Krista needed her rest.

"I saw a man," Krista mentioned.

Standing at the doorway, Maggie inquired, "Oh yeah?"

"Yeah, it was weird. I saw a dark man with an umbrella."

"Oh," Maggie encouraged her to continue. But, Maggie finally understood what Krista had been trying to tell her.

"He was very familiar, like I knew him," Krista shook her head. She pulled her arms into her like she was giving herself a hug.

Maggie waited for Krista to say more. But, it appeared she was finished talking for now. Her eyes glazed over as she stared into the distance. She slid one leg up the bed and wrapped her arms around it while she rested her chin on her knee. Then, her gaze slowly dropped to the floor. Maggie's heart sunk looking at the little girl who looked so sad. She had just been through a war and had almost been a casualty. The saddest part about it was she didn't even know why.

Chapter XIII

"Are you sure about that," Chris asked the other person on the phone. "So, there's no record at all of me being married?"

He listened to what he was being told. But, he just shook his head. It was his imagination playing serious tricks on him. It wasn't any call for concern. But, it did bother him. It all felt so real.

"Thanks anyway Janet," Chris said as he put down the phone.

His little Angel who had been inspiring him to paint paintings of her seemed so real. But then, the feelings had become so strong for the lady Angel called her mother. Chris reasoned that there was an entire life, about which he knew nothing at all. But, there had to be memories and thoughts from his other world. These could be it! He just didn't have any connection to it.

He had to be able to tap into that part of his mind somehow. So, Chris started thinking that he had constructed Angel to become his messenger. She was telling him things that only his subconscious knew. He couldn't make those connections any other way.

But, Janet had done her research. She went back twenty years to find no record of Chris being married. She checked the database of records and went back as far as she could. Where the database ended, she started to research physical documents in filing cabinets that had been moved to the basement and shoved in a corner years ago. They were so old, they had collected dust. But, there was no record at all.

Janet had done some really extensive research. But, what they were missing was that Chris hadn't lived his entire life in Fredericksburg, Virginia. They had no idea of knowing. Knowing that would have answered many of their questions.

Chris tried to paint Angel and her mother. But, it presented a unique obstacle. By the time he hung his easel on the porch and had his paint ready, his memory of the lady was hazy. He tried everything to get her back. He read the poem and looked at all the other paintings of Angel. But, he just couldn't conjure those visions as clearly again.

He painted it anyway. He decided to just go with it. Painting Angel was easy. She was sitting in front of her mother with a bright smile on her face. But when it came to painting the lady in the background, there was very little detail.

Stepping back from what he had painted, Chris looked it over and felt the omen. He didn't know the lady and had no idea who she was. He had come to know Angel and felt a strong connection with her. But, the ghost that stood behind her was someone he didn't know.

It was an interesting juxtaposition. His last two paintings had taken on a new style. The first painting of Angel was merely an outlined image, a sad girl with no life in her. In his latest painting, she was bright, smiling and happy. But the lady behind her was now merely an outlined image, a transparent spirit with very little definition. Putting the two paintings side by side in his secret room, they made an interesting juxtaposition indeed.

Krista had been walking around the house like a zombie for days. She was quiet and very reflective. Maggie had noticed the change in Krista's character. But, it was understandable for a little girl who had just been through such an ordeal.

In her bare feet and her sun dress, she seemed to float around the house. Looking out the front window, she took a seat and stared for hours. Then, she moved to the back porch and sat down on the steps. Looking out over the backyard, past the barn, she realized she had never ventured out that far.

Maggie kept her eye on Krista. But when Krista started to journey through the yard, Maggie didn't think anything of it. She didn't question it at all. Krista herself really didn't fully comprehend what she was doing. She just started walking.

The edge of the yard was lined with trees, but it didn't start into deep woods. It was just a line of dogwoods that opened up into a pasture with tall grass and a few blooming buckeyes. Krista stretched out her arms and let the grass brush her hands as she walked across the pasture to the old abandoned dirt road on the other side.

Crossing the road, she ventured further until she came to a bank where she could hear the rush of white water. There was a path that led down to the rocky bank where she took a seat and admired the water rushing by her. She had never been this far alone. It was a beautiful place with high standing trees on the other side of the river. They were turning colors and the browns, yellows and oranges were amazing signs of what nature can do when it puts its mind to it.

Chris had decided a long time ago that painting on his porch just wasn't good enough anymore, at least not every time. He could see a vision in his head. But, it might be better to have the subject in front of him while he painted. That way, he could really bring it to life.

So, he grabbed his easel and canvas. Putting them in the truck, he had no idea where he was going to take them. But, he knew he had plenty of land to explore. He'd find a place!

He headed into town to get some perspective, but the system of highways got a little daunting as he took an off-ramp and found himself on an even bigger highway. He definitely had made the wrong turn somewhere. Finally finding a nice quiet road, he drove for miles until he turned down a dirt road. Chris thought to himself, "Now, I'm getting somewhere."

To his left, he could see rushing water and beautiful high trees in the distance. Chris drove on for a few more miles until he found a place to park, but he was quite sure he had just found his next subject.

Chris hadn't noticed because he was heavily enthralled by the mountain sitting pleasantly across the river from where he had setup his canvas. But after he had started painting is when he noticed her sitting there admiring the same view. She was a few hundred feet up the bank and he only noticed because he took his eyes off the river to mix some more paint.

His heart nearly leapt out of his chest. Her likeness was exactly his Angel. But, there was something different about her this time. She seemed more real than she ever did and she wasn't paying any attention to him. Was his mind playing tricks on him again or was she real?

Krista could feel someone staring at her. When she turned to look, she was surprised to see a man painting on the side of the bank. It made sense though. Who wouldn't want to paint this beautiful mountain and rushing waters captivating them both?

But, there was something very familiar about him. He was in the distance and the shade from the trees behind him darkened his silhouette. She felt like she had seen him before. She couldn't remember when or where. But, she knew. She just knew she had seen him somewhere else.

As she was staring at him, it was as if he could feel her eyes and he turned away. While she kept staring at his side profile, she felt a growing connection. She looked at the river and then back at him. Déjà vu can play some awfully interesting tricks on a person's mind. It was playing one on Krista's.

The river was familiar. The man was familiar. The entire picture she was viewing was familiar. But, she was quite sure she had never been to the river before. She didn't know the man, and she didn't trust what she was thinking anyway.

Chapter XIV

Chris had four paintings waiting patiently for Amy when she finally decided to come get them. But, his furniture design was going to have to wait. Chris was still painting.

He had a beautiful picture in his mind and it wouldn't let go. The girl on the river looked so much like his Angel that he had to paint that scene. He was well aware of the fact that while he was painting her, she hadn't come to visit yet. It was something he thought of briefly and thought a bit strange. But, he kept painting. The image was too strong.

She startled him because his mind was in another world, "You paint portraits too?"

Chris turned to see Amy standing there admiring his art. World's were colliding. Secrets were being revealed. Chris thought quick, "I'm giving it a try!"

"Well, it's beautiful," Amy reassured him.

Chris looked back at the painting and tried to view it with fresh eyes. It *was* beautiful. But, he knew he was biased. He couldn't possibly see it the way anyone else saw it.

"You should paint more," Amy continued.

If she only knew was the thought that went across Chris's mind. But, this was going to create an interesting dilemma. Chris knew that Amy was going to want to sell it. How would Chris get away with not giving it to her?

Finally Amy broke his train of thought with an entirely different conversation, "Chris I have been meaning to ask you."

"What?"

"You know the furniture that you build," Amy asked.

"I have a general knowledge of it, yes," Chris answered.

Amy laughed. "Would you want to sell any of the pieces," Amy asked.

"I already do," Chris answered.

"Well yeah," Amy continued. "But, I mean in a store."

Chris thought about that for a second. "What do you mean, like in a department store?"

"Uh, no," Amy answered. "I have been talking to some of the smaller stores around town and I can get your furniture placed in those stores on consignment. It would open up your furniture sales past the orders that you're getting now."

"So, I would have to start building my furniture faster," Chris asked.

"Actually," Amy had come prepared, "You wouldn't."

"How so?"

"I contacted a manufacturer who would take the pieces you design and recreate them," Amy answered. "He would be able to produce your furniture, the pieces that are very popular. All you would have to do is just keep designing furniture and leave the rest up to me."

Chris put his paint brush down and grabbed his cup of coffee. He had already past the thought of telling Amy it was a great idea. He was already coming up with names, "My Unique Series."

"What," Amy asked.

"That's what I'll call it," Chris answered.

A huge smile came across Amy's face, "So, you'll do it?"

"Sure," Chris answered. "This is huge! I love it!"

Amy jumped and clapped. Then, she looked Chris dead in the eyes, "I'll be right back!"

Amy ran out to her car and grabbed a bottle of champagne. She returned and handed it to Chris. Chris looked it over, "So you knew I was going to say yes?"

"Um, actually I didn't," Amy answered. "I was hoping!"

Gilmer came flying in the front door looking for Maggie, "Mag! Mag! Where are you?"

"Where do you think I am Gil," Maggie answered from the kitchen.

Gilmer was standing in the middle of the living room looking up the steps, "Oh."

Gilmer walked into the kitchen and looked straight at Maggie with a look of surprise. "Well, what is it," Maggie asked.

"You would not believe what I just found out," Gilmer announced.

"Ok," Maggie went back to doing what she was doing.

"No, seriously," Gilmer said.

"Oh, alright Gil," Maggie looked at Gilmer and gave him her full attention. "What did you just find out?"

"They have a job that you catch animals," Gilmer answered.

Maggie stared at Gilmer stunned, "Yeah honey, they've had that for years."

"You've known about the job where you catch animals," Gilmer asked.

"Well sure," Maggie answered.

"Well, why didn't you tell me," Gilmer asked.

"You never asked," Maggie answered.

"Well, what else haven't you told me," Gilmer wondered.

"Well, let me see," Maggie responded. "They have people who fly planes and they've got people who give you electricity too. But, we never had those conversations either."

Gilmer stood staring at Maggie with his hands on his hips, "Well, I knew all that."

By then, Krista had come down the stairs and was walking into the kitchen.

Gilmer looked at her, "Did you know that they have a job where you catch animals all day?"

"Um yeah," Krista answered. "They're called animal catchers."

"You too," Gilmer replied in shock. "You've got to be kidding me!"

"Well, what brought all this on Gil," Maggie asked.

Gilmer looked at Maggie and a big smile crept across his face, "I'm going to be one!"

"You're kidding," Maggie answered.

"Yeah," Gilmer continued. "I was just talking a guy who works over there and he said he could get me a job."

"You're serious," Maggie recognized.

"Yeah," Gilmer reassured her. "I'm going to go around catching animals all day."

"Well, that will be the life of you then," Maggie shook her head.

"What do you mean," Gilmer asked.

"Oh, never mind," Maggie answered. "You have fun crawling underneath porches and crawling through crawl spaces under the house to find things that bite and have rabies and stuff."

"Yeah," Gilmer cheered. "That's the fun part."

"Eww," Krista said. "You like all that stuff?"

"Well yeah," Gilmer answered. "They even said they have bombs that we set off from time to time."

"He was pulling your leg Gil," Maggie answered.

"Bombs," Krista's face lit up with excitement. "What kind of bombs?"

"I don't know," Gilmer answered. "I can't wait to use one though. I'm going to get 'em good!"

"Yeah, you do that honey," Maggie said mockingly.

Krista stared at Gilmer with excitement, "I can do the bomb part. But, I wouldn't want to crawl under someone's house where a rat pooped and a snake might have laid its eggs."

Gilmer stopped and stared at Krista for a second. He hadn't thought of the good points she had just made. He pondered for a moment, and then shot it all down, "They give us special suits to wear."

"Wow dad," Krista shook her head.

"I don't care if they gave me full body armor, I wouldn't do it," Maggie laughed.

Gilmer nodded his head, "It comes with benefits!"

Maggie stopped what she was doing and stared at Gilmer for a moment, "Well then, you go get that job."

"Thought that would change your mind," Gilmer responded with a huge smile on his face.

Chapter XV

Gilmer was standing in the kitchen staring at Maggie, "She will be turning sixteen this year. She'll want her permit soon. I was able to put her down for medical insurance. But, that was just the form. They are going to want her information. What are we going to do?"

"Gil," Maggie answered, "I thought about that a long time ago when she was sick." Maggie walked into the living room where she had her roll top desk. That's where she kept track of the bills and stored special documents.

She pulled an envelope out and handed it to Gilmer. Gilmer opened it and started fingering through the documents. There was a birth certificate and a social security card, both with "Kissy Seiler" on them.

Gilmer's eyes grew wide, "So, she's like really our daughter."

"It's official," Maggie answered.

"How did you do this," Gilmer asked.

"I found a site on the internet," Maggie answered.

"Internet? Where did you get on the internet," Gilmer asked.

"At the library," Maggie answered.

"And you can just get stuff like this on the internet," Gilmer asked.

"Well, it wasn't that easy. I had to look pretty hard," Maggie answered. "But once I found the site, all I needed was a credit card and we were in business."

"Um, what? Where did you get the credit card," Gilmer asked.

Maggie laughed, "Gilmer, it is funny how much you don't know. I got it at the store. It's not really a credit card. You put money on it and you can use it like one."

"Oh, so," Gilmer thought, "You're spending money that you put on it?"

"Well yeah," Maggie confirmed what Gilmer was thinking. "It seems stupid. But, the card comes in handy, especially for something like this."

Gilmer nodded slowly as he looked at Maggie. All of this new information was registering, but it was taking its time. Then all of a sudden, a bright smile came across his face, "She's finally really ours!"

"Yep, Gilmer," Maggie smiled back, "She sure is!"

Dust flew as the truck barreled down the road. The truck flew past the line of trees and the old fence that marked the property. She turned the corner, but with much better control than she had back when she was fourteen. She was much safer and more stable with her driving.

Maggie watched as Krista approached the driveway and turned into the yard. Grabbing her hand towel off of her shoulder, she climbed down the porch steps and started across the yard. Krista jumped out of the truck and ran over to Maggie excited.

"I got my license," Krista yelled in excitement. "I got my license."

"I know honey," Maggie laughed. "You wouldn't be driving if you didn't."

Krista gave Maggie a hug while jumping up and down in excitement. Gilmer climbed out of the passenger side of the truck and walked over to the other two. "Yeah, she did real good the guy said. Didn't make any major mistakes or anything."

"Well good," Maggie said smiling.

"Yeah, I nailed the parallel parking," Krista confirmed.

"Wow," Maggie exclaimed. "It took you the longest time to learn that. I can't even do that."

Krista stopped hugging Maggie and thought about it for a second, "I didn't know you drove."

"Oh, I don't drive much," Maggie answered. "I only drive when I have to and I haven't had to for about," Maggie stopped to scratch her head, "Well, it must be about ten years now."

"What," Krista asked.

"Yep, sounds about right," Gilmer included.

Maggie clapped her hands together as she stared straight at Krista, "I've got a surprise for you."

Krista's face lit up with excitement, "You do?"

"Yes we do," Gilmer added.

Krista covered her face with her hands, "What is it?"

"Gilmer, go get it," Maggie ordered.

"Yes, ma'am," Gilmer answered. With that, he walked around to the other side of the house.

Maggie grabbed Krista's hand and Krista looked over at her making a note that she had never seen her mother so happy. She had seen her in a good mood. But, Maggie was excited and really enjoying what was to come. It made Krista feel strange.

That's when she heard it. From the other side of the house, she could hear the roar of something new. Looking at Maggie and then back to the house, she thought, "What in the world?"

Maggie looked at Krista and tightened her hand. Then, she felt the need to start explaining, "Now, it's not the best. We couldn't afford the best. But, it's something we thought you could use."

"No you didn't," Krista said as a big smile crept across her face.

"Yes we did," Maggie answered with a huge smile of her own.

That's when she could see it. It wasn't the ugliest car in the world. It had its rust spots and what color was showing was a dull blue. But in Krista's eyes, it was the most beautiful car she had ever seen.

Gilmer drove it around the house and right up to where Krista was standing. She stood stunned for a moment. Then, she started to explore. Gilmer got out of the driver's seat so that Krista could get in it.

She adjusted the seat and the mirrors just as she had been instructed. Then, she looked at the tape deck and laughed. Gilmer bent over and looked in the car.

"What's funny," he asked.

"The tape deck," Krista answered.

"What? Having a tape deck was the thing in my day," Gilmer responded.

"I don't even think they have tapes anymore Gil," Maggie joined.

"Oh," Gilmer thought.

"No biggie," Krista said. "Hey look, there's a tape in it." She handed it to Gilmer.

"Pit House," Gilmer yelled as he read the band on the tape.

"Who," Krista asked.

"Pit House," Gilmer repeated. "They were the band!"

"Never heard of them," Krista shook her head.

"Don't worry honey," Maggie joined. "Neither have I."

Krista and Maggie shared a laugh. Gilmer shoved the tape in his pocket, "I'll just keep it then."

"Ok," without any hesitation from Krista.

"Yeah, she's not worried about that old tape," Maggie confirmed. "But, we have other stuff to talk about."

Krista looked up at Maggie wondering what she meant. Gilmer looked at Maggie nodding his head. "Yeah, yeah," Gilmer confirmed, "We have to talk to you about the car."

"Ok," Krista looked worried.

"Well, we bought the car," Maggie mentioned. "It passed inspection and everything. So, we got the tags and it's all legal. We even got insurance, but there will be another payment in a month."

"Ok," Krista nodded her head.

"Well, the thing is," Gilmer continued. "We can't afford it."

"Oh," Krista nodded. She patted the steering wheel and looked around the car like she was taking a last look. Krista had always done a great job at hiding her disappointment. But, Maggie could see it and Gilmer knew it too.

"But, I have a solution honey," Maggie continued.

"Oh, yeah," Krista looked up at Maggie with bright eyes.

"Yeah," Maggie confirmed. "All you have to do is get a job in that time and then take over the insurance payments yourself."

"Can I," Krista asked.

"Well sure," Gilmer answered. "You're sixteen now and you have a car," Gilmer pointed out the obvious.

"I can have a job when I'm sixteen," Krista asked.

"I think so," Maggie answered.

"Yeah," Gilmer said. "I think that's the going rate!"

Krista looked back at the inside of the car and felt the seats. Her smile was still bright and contagious, "Well then, I will start job hunting."

"Great," Maggie answered.

Maggie and Gilmer were both relieved. They had never asked Krista for anything. But, they knew that the time had come when Krista could start paying her own way for certain things. They weren't going to make her do it all. But, starting with asking her to pay her own insurance wasn't all that terrible.

Chapter XVI

With his furniture in the stores downtown, Chris thought one day it would be nice to see it for himself. He hardly ever ventured downtown. He liked to keep to himself on his farm with only the interaction of people like Amy and his very few furniture customers.

But, actually seeing his furniture in a store got him excited. Plus, he was interested in seeing the quality of work the manufacturer could do. When he worked on them himself, his pieces were handcrafted and some of it took him an extremely long amount of time to put together.

Chris was very interested in taking a look at one of his designs to see how the manufacturer was able to put more than a hundred pieces together in a week. It was all very new to him. Chris was really looking forward to what this next chapter in his life was going to bring.

As he walked around the store, he spotted his pieces right away. They were placed in different parts of the room and they blended in with their surroundings quite nicely. As he examined his bench, a clerk of the store walked up to him.

"Can I help you sir?"

Chris looked up at her, "Oh, well I was just looking at this piece right here."

"Um yes," the clerk grew a wide smile. "Actually, I have a feeling these are going to be very popular. You are the third person who has asked me about it today. This is a piece designed by Chris Ferlin. It has no specific name. It's just called His Bench. But, we have his other pieces that come from his Unique Series like the Legless over here," the clerk pointed to the corner as she mentioned it.

Chris followed the clerk's direction. Looking around the room to see where the Legless had been placed, he nodded as he walked toward it. The clerk followed him.

"Are you interested in this one sir," the clerk asked.

"Actually, I am," Chris answered. "I'd like to take a closer look."

Chris pulled it toward him and placed it facing down while the clerk continued to talk, "It's called the Legless because the designer figured out a way to make a chair with no legs."

Chris was studying the binding in the back, "That's exactly right."

The clerk looked at Chris cocking her head and raising an eyebrow, "Well if you're interested, let me get your information. What is your name?"

Chris stood up and put his hand out for the clerk to shake, "I'm Chris Ferlin."

The clerk looked at him stunned. Then, she looked at the chair and back at him, "You're Mr. Ferlin? Amy told me you lived somewhere around here. But, I didn't know you would be dropping in."

"Yes, I'm Chris," he answered. "I just wanted to see my work."

"Well, what do you think," the clerk asked laughing off her anxiety. "My name is Shell by the way."

"Hi Shell," Chris acknowledged. "Nice to meet you. I am happy. I definitely like the work put into these chairs."

"The owner is going to be so excited you stopped in to see your work," Shell mentioned.

As Chris let out a slight laugh, the lady who had been standing behind him interrupted their conversation, "You designed these chairs?"

Chris turned to look at her, "Uh yes, hi, I'm Chris Ferlin."

"Wow! You're Chris Ferlin, like on the tag. Well, ain't that something. My name is Maggie, Maggie Seiler. I was just admiring your work."

"Great," Chris answered. "I'm glad you like it. I have more pieces too."

"Oh yes," Shell interrupted. "He does. And he painted these paintings as well," Shell continued as she pointed around at several of the paintings on the walls.

"You painted these paintings too," Maggie asked in astonishment.

"Yes, I did," Chris answered. "I've been doing landscapes and a few other different types for years. But, mainly landscapes."

"Well every time I've come in here," Maggie said, "I've been wanting to get one of your paintings. But…"

"I know," Chris affirmed, "They are a bit pricey." Chris looked at Maggie hard, purely unintentional.

Maggie nodded with a crooked smile. It made Chris's heart melt when he saw that his words had hit a little deep.

"Um, tell you what," Chris had a thought. "You can have one."

Maggie's eyes grew bright, "Really?"

"Yes," Chris confirmed, "Absolutely!"

"Um, Mr. Ferlin," Shell interrupted.

"No, it's ok," Chris knew what Shell wanted to say. "Amy will handle everything. Let's give Mrs. uh Seiler a painting."

Maggie practically ran across the street. Krista never saw her move so fast. Then, she noticed the painting in Maggie's hand, "What is that?"

"Oh, you would not believe," Maggie answered with excitement. "I just met the painter of this here painting."

"You did," Krista asked.

"Yeah," Maggie answered. "He was right there in that store." As Maggie pointed across the street toward the store, she saw him, "That's him. That's the painter right there."

As Chris watched Maggie cross the street, it caught his eye when she started pointing back at him. Then, his world came to a sudden halt as he saw the girl. It was the girl from the river. She was real!

Krista was staring straight back at Chris. It felt to both of them like an eternity. They were locked in a stare and they didn't even realize it.

Krista recognized the man from the river. But she also saw the man from the silhouette, if only she could remember where she saw the man from the silhouette. The world faded around him and her vision was like she was looking at him through a tunnel.

Chris not only was locked in a stare with Krista, but he was also having visions of the house behind her. There was something very familiar about it. He broke his stare to take in a full view of the home.

Up the street was a marketplace where plenty of people were walking in all different directions. Down the street was just a corner that turned the road and took it out of sight. When Chris looked back at the house, Krista had already gotten in her car and was getting ready to drive away. With one last glance, she looked at him again. Then, she drove down the street and around the corner.

When Maggie and Krista walked in the house, Krista went straight to the steps. Maggie looked at her weird, "You gonna help me find a place for this here painting?"

But, Krista just waved her hand as she kept walking up the steps. Maggie followed her with her eyes and then shook her head, "I wish I knew half the time what got into that poor girl. Ever since she got sick that last time, she's been acting different."

"You don't say," Gilmer announced. He had been sitting on the couch. But, he stood up in the middle of the living room and looked down at what Maggie had in her hand, "Whatcha got there?"

Maggie looked down at her hand, and then she looked up with a huge smile, "I got this painting from the guy who painted it!"

As Maggie went on about the painting and the experience of meeting the actual painter, Krista could hear everything she was saying from upstairs. But, she walked to her room like she was excited about something herself. She climbed up on her bed. But then, she reached down and started pulling things out from under it.

Underneath her bed, Krista had a sketchpad and a stack of drawings. They were all scribble sketches of a dark silhouette. In most of them, the silhouette appeared to be a tall man with an umbrella. But in one of the sketches, he was a painter on the bank of a river.

Krista had a unique style when it came to scribbling her sketches. With the sketchpad resting on her knees, her hands flew around the paper only touching when she felt the outline of what she was drawing. She would run her pencil over the same line several times until she felt moved to a different part of the picture.

Her scribbles were calculated. But, her speed was remarkable. She scribbled away until finally she had the drawing of the man across the street. She circled him several times and then shaded the outside to give the picture a funnel perspective.

Staring at her picture, she wondered what these flashbacks were. The guy she saw at the river certainly looked exactly like the guy she saw across the street downtown. And that would make sense because he too was a painter.

But, she didn't know him and it gave her an eerie feeling that he reminded her of the silhouette flashbacks she had been having for quite some time. The thing is that he was very familiar. It gave her a sense of peace in a world of uncertainty.

Chapter XVII

Chris had been coming in the diner for a while now. Once he started exploring downtown Fredericksburg, especially in the Historic District where his furniture was a hit, Chris eyed a diner that had the vintage look he liked. What attracted his attention was its simplicity.

The signs on the front and sides of the diner were modestly marked "Restaurant" and "Eat Here." How could anyone mistake what they could find in there? That was Chris's type of place.

So, he had started to visit the diner rather regularly. He would come in once or twice a week, and the waitresses would swap covering his table. After all, he was a very good tipper and it's only courteous for them to spread the wealth.

Chris had just ordered his coffee and the waitress gave him more time to look over the menu when he heard a voice mention his name. Looking around, he saw a very well-dressed lady staring straight at him. Cocking his head, he waited to hear if he had heard her correctly.

"Mr. Chris Ferlin," she asked again.

"Yes ma'am," Chris answered.

"I'm Jamie Trenton from Line and Edge Magazine."

"Line and Edge," Chris asked.

"Uh, yes sir," Jamie answered. "Do you mind if I join you?"

"Um, no. Not at all," Chris answered with slight hesitation.

Jamie sat down and slid into the booth. Then, she looked square at Chris with a bright beaming smile. Chris felt a little uneasy until Jamie spoke, "I've been dying to do an article on you. I just finally got them to clear it."

"Who," Chris asked.

"What," Jamie responded.

"Who are they? The them," Chris clarified.

"Oh," Jamie understood. "I write for Line and Edge Magazine. We are an art magazine. We cover all kinds of art and I heard about you years ago when, well it's a long story, but a friend of mine is a friend of a friend of Milley Montagne."

"Hmm," Chris wondered.

"Milley Montagne," Jamie looked shocked.

Chris shook his head absolutely clueless. The waitress arrived with Chris's coffee and asked what Jamie would like to have.

"Oh, I'll have the same," Jamie ordered.

"Great," the waitress answered and started to walk away. Then, she turned back to Chris, "Oh by the way, Milley Montagne is a huge actress in Hollywood. She did movies like Sandbox Hill and The Yearbook Mansion."

"Really," Chris responded, still a little confused. But, now his confusion was why Milley Montagne had anything to do with his life or his art.

The waitress continued to stand at the table with the look on her face that begged the obvious question, to which Jamie couldn't wait to respond, "Oh, one of his paintings was bought by Milley."

The expression on the waitress's face immediately changed to amazement, "You are kidding me!"

"No, I am not," Jamie confirmed. "In fact, there are many celebrities who have bought his paintings. It became an insider's secret."

The waitress touched Chris's shoulder and joked that she had just touched someone famous. Jamie egged her on energetically. But in all the fun they were having, they had completely missed that Chris was stunned and speechless.

Chris had let Amy handle all the business. He didn't ask questions and she didn't volunteer, out of respect for what she had concluded was one of his quirks. But, Amy had been paying Chris rather handsomely and he should have known there was something about that.

When the waitress returned with Jamie's coffee, she hung around to listen to the interview. Neither Chris nor Jamie minded at all. No one else did either since their table was the only one their waitress had to cover. In fact, the diner only had a handful of patrons left in it anyway.

So, Jamie reached in her bag and pulled out a notebook. Then, she began, "So, what inspires your art?"

Chris stared at Jamie for a second while the waitress took a seat in the table next to them, "I don't know. I guess it started as therapy. I had a vision in my head one day and I was trying to get it out."

"Why was it so important to you," Jamie pressed.

Chris nodded his head and then began, "Well, I had been in a coma for about nine years…"

"You were in a coma," Jamie asked surprised.

The waitress had gained company by this time when another waitress had finished off her last table. They both sighed in unison.

"Uh yes, for nine years," Chris answered.

Jamie and the two waitresses melted with looks of concern in their eyes. Then, Jamie continued, "So, you were trying to capture something with your art?"

"Yes, it was a vision that was so real," Chris looked at Jamie with the most honest expression.

"A vision," Jamie repeated.

"Well yeah, see the thing was I couldn't remember anything from before the coma," Chris further informed.

Jamie and the two waitresses were completely astounded. When Jamie looked over at the other two, they could only shake their heads and shrug. Then, she whispered, "What was the vision?"

Chris thought long and deep about his answer. He looked out the window for the words to say. But, he hadn't talked about it to anyone. He had no idea where to begin to talk about an Angel who had been haunting him, "It was a picture of a river."

"Why," Jamie asked. "Why would that have been so important to you?"

"I thought maybe it was a connection to another time and place. Something that would bring back my memory and help me figure out who I was," Chris spoke passionately about the underlying truth to it all. But, he would not speak of her. Letting his secret go would be acknowledging she didn't exist.

    The interview continued as Chris spun the truth around the omission of his Angel. Their talk had gained a bit more attention. All of the waitresses were seated at the table nearest Chris and Jamie. The handful of patrons in the diner were enjoying their coffee and listening intently as well.

    A final question Jamie asked concluded their interview, "Where do you see yourself going with your art?"

    "I have never really thought about it Jamie," Chris reflected. "It has been a good ride and I'll just keep moving where my heart moves me. I mean, it's what got me here right? Why change anything now?"

    Jamie lingered on Chris's last words for an awkward moment, "Ok, thank you."

Everyone in the diner started applauding. That's when Chris realized everyone's attention had been turned to him. With a humble smile on his face, he acknowledged everyone around the room. Then, he looked for his waitress.

"Can I get a refill," he said as he raised his cup.

His waitress softly clapped as she cocked her head and whispered, "You were great!" Then, she stood up and grabbed his cup.

Chapter XVIII

"Chris! Chris," Amy stood in the middle of his living room. She had been yelling for a minute.

Chris came flying through the back door thinking there was an emergency, "What's wrong? What's going on?"

"Oh, there you are," Amy turned around to face Chris.

"Yeah, what's wrong," Chris asked.

"Nothing," Amy answered. "Nothing's wrong. Just wondering where you are. Where were you?"

"Oh, out back working on something," Chris answered.

"Oh yeah," Amy asked with interest. "What are you working on now?"

Chris laughed to himself looking at Amy's inquisitive smile, "I'm building myself a bigger workshop to design more elaborate pieces of furniture and maybe branch out into other stuff."

"You want to branch out into other stuff," Amy raised an eyebrow.

"Well, I haven't thought of anything yet," Chris answered. "But, I'm getting ready just in case. I do feel something might be brewing in this little mind of mine. Don't worry! You'll be the first to know."

Amy laughed, "Oh by the way, did you get a visitor the other day?"

"Yeah," Chris answered surprised. "How did you know?"

"I sent her," Amy announced. "She called me because she knew I dealt your art and I told her where you might be."

"Yep," Chris responded. "She found me there."

"So, how did it go," Amy asked.

"I think it went well," Chris answered as he started toward the kitchen. "I think I learned more than she did though."

"Oh yeah," Amy asked as she followed Chris to the kitchen. "How so?"

"Well, it appears I'm an Insider's Secret among celebrities," Chris joked.

"You're a what," Amy truly didn't understand the term.

"Yeah, that was my reaction," Chris agreed. "Did you know that some of my paintings have been bought by celebrities?" Chris handed Amy a cup of coffee.

"Oh yeah," Amy perked up as she answered. "Your work is loved and admired in Hollywood! That's what they mean by the Insider's Secret?"

"Uh, yes," Chris answered. "It seems they have been buying my paintings for years."

"I know Chris," Amy said. "I've been selling it to them."

"I had no idea," Chris remarked.

"Well, you don't ask a whole lot of questions," Amy answered the unasked question.

"I know. I just found it pretty cool," Chris mentioned. "In fact, everyone at the diner thought it was cool."

"Oh yeah," Amy responded.

"Yeah," Chris continued, "Jamie and I, Jamie was her name, her and I had quite the audience when she was finished asking questions."

Amy laughed. She looked at Chris while she drank her coffee, "Did she tell you when the article would come out?"

Chris recalled, "She said a few months. I'm not really sure."

"Well," Amy remarked, "It's a good thing."

Chris stood at the kitchen bar giving Amy a look. Then, he nodded before taking a sip of his coffee. Amy tried to study what might be going on in Chris's mind. But, she had learned over the years that would never happen.

Gilmer walked in the front door and placed his jacket on the chair as he strolled into the kitchen with his cooler, "Hey, guess what I got today!"

"What," Maggie asked.

"A couple snakes under one guy's porch and then guess what else," Gilmer urged again.

"Oh, what Gil," Maggie answered.

"A whole bunch of bats in another guy's barn," Gilmer said with excitement.

"See," Maggie raised her voice, "One of these days you're gonna get bit."

"We don't get bit Mag," Gilmer assured. "We are professionals. We know what we're doing."

"You haven't even been doing that job for a year now," Maggie reminded.

"But, it feels like I've been doing it all my life," Gilmer reassured her. "And come to think of it, I have too. I've been fighting critters underneath the house since before I could drive."

"That's not the same Gil," Maggie thought.

"Why not," Gilmer asked. "What makes that any different?"

Maggie thought long and hard. There were no answers to Gilmer's question.

A smile beamed across Gilmer's face, "Awe, you're worried about me." Gilmer started walking toward Maggie with his arms stretched wide.

"No. No. No," Maggie said with authority. "You need to go scrub yourself first. Come at me with that!"

Gilmer was laughing hard as Krista walked in the kitchen. She stood at the door with her hands on her hips, "What's funny?"

Gilmer stopped laughing long enough to answer, "Oh, your mother don't like the fact that I climbed underneath a house for snakes and then chased bats out of another guy's barn."

"Really," Krista said surprised. "You better watch out with the bats though. I mean, snakes aren't anything to play with either. But, you can get rabies from those bats. Come to think of it, just be careful with all of it. The raccoons the other week, the skunks that one time, none of it's any good."

"Awe, you care too," Gilmer started toward Krista with his arms outstretched.

"Oh no. No. No. No," Krista wagged her finger. "You need a shower first dad."

"Yeah dad," Maggie mocked. "Go scrub the rabies off ya."

Gilmer laughed and put down his arms. Then, he whispered to Krista, "Did you get that thing done I asked?"

Krista looked up at Gilmer and nodded silently.

"Good," Gilmer whispered. "Good girl!"

As Gilmer walked away, Maggie eyed Krista. Then Maggie cocked her head, "What was that about?"

"Nothing," Krista answered with a slight rise to her voice.

"What are you two plotting," Maggie asked with a suspicious tone.

Krista looked at Maggie with a suspicious glare, "Don't you worry about it."

"Uh huh," Maggie raised her eyebrow. "Better not be up to nothing good."

"You'll know soon enough," Krista suggested as she gave Maggie a knowing glance before looking out the window.

Maggie studied Krista for a moment, "I don't know what I'm going to do with you two."

Chapter XIX

Chris had started to make sketches of paintings he was going to do. It was a way for him to put together a blueprint of what painting he was about to do next. Mountains, country roads and rivers had all started to look the same to him. He definitely was looking for a way to take his art to the next level.

Years ago, he had started doing buildings. But, he was too shy back then to sit his easel on the sidewalk and paint the building across the street. What he would do is take a mental picture of the building he wanted to paint and then he would give it a try at home. But, he missed so much detail that way.

It was time for him to start getting up, close and personal with his subjects. But, he had stages to his work. His stages included taking a few photos with his phone. Then, he'd go to the diner and sketch it. That way he could get a feel for the painting and he would know exactly where he had to start.

He was working on one such sketch at the diner when she suddenly startled him. Tapping Chris on the shoulder, she walked around announcing, "I was looking for you."

Chris turned his head to see Amy already passing him and taking a seat across from him in the booth, "Well, I have been here."

Amy grabbed the sketchpad and started to look over the sketches, "Hey, you're doing sketches now?"

"No, not really," Chris answered. "I mean, I do sketches. But, only as a pre-planning stage to an actual painting."

"Oh, you are going to paint this," Amy asked.

"Yes," Chris answered. "I'm doing the beginning work for it now."

"I like how you sketch," Amy admired. "Your scribbles are very calculated. I can see you jumping around the page from point to point, very fast. But then, you work on an area for a minute before moving to the next. Nice technique!"

"Thank you," Chris nodded truly appreciating the compliments.

"Oh, you bet," Amy said. "I love all your artwork. Speaking of which, that's why I came to bother you. What did you ever do with that portrait?"

Chris thought hard about what Amy could possibly mean. When he shook his head, Amy took her cue.

She continued, "The one day I saw you painting a portrait of a blonde girl?"

Chris thought longer and harder. Then, he remembered. But, he couldn't tell her about that painting. He couldn't let those worlds collide. Amy could have everything else, but he was not going to give up his Angel, "Amy, that was a few years ago."

"Oh, I know," Amy responded. "Sometimes I get so busy and then I forget stuff. But, early this morning I remembered. Well, I finally remembered. I guess it was one of those out of sight out of mind things. But, it dawned on me that you hadn't sent that painting over."

Chris had to think of an answer. He needed one that would be good enough for Amy, because he had tried to lie to her before and he wasn't that good at it. Something came to him that she might understand and not question, "I never finished that."

"You didn't finish it," Amy questioned.

Chris nodded his head, "Yeah, I couldn't find the feel for painting a portrait. I couldn't bring her to life. So, I painted something else over it."

"Oh, I can't even see it," Amy asked.

Chris was feeling the flow of his lie, "You've already sold it."

"Well, that's a shame," Amy stated.

"Not really," Chris responded.

Amy's eyes grew wide as she craned her neck to see. She raised an eyebrow as she murmured, "It's uncanny."

Chris looked at her, "What is?"

"That girl," Amy nodded. "She looks just like the girl that was in your painting, the one we were just talking about."

Chris's expression lost all life, "What?"

He turned his head and looked around the room. It took him a second to find her and his heart started racing. But, his waitress saw him looking and came to his service.

Blocking his view of Angel, she asked, "Yes, Chris? Need a refill?"

Chris looked up at his waitress, "Um yeah, sure!"

"Chris. Chris," Amy tried to catch Chris's attention.

Chris turned around and nodded at her, "Mm hmm?"

Amy patted him on his hands and then rose to her feet, "Ok. I am going to go." Then she looked at the young girl who had caught Chris's undivided attention, "That should give you motivation to try again." Amy winked and walked away, touching Chris's shoulder as she left.

Chris looked back toward Angel. He was glad to see that she hadn't left yet. But, he was interrupted again as his waitress brought the coffee to the table and started pouring, "Would you like dessert?"

"Hmm," Chris asked.

"Dessert? Would you like some dessert," the waitress repeated.

"Um," Chris was thinking. But, it was the slow kind of thinking that clearly indicated there was something else on his mind.

The waitress looked in the general direction where Chris was staring. When Kissy caught her eye, she immediately understood, "Oh Chris, you want to meet the new waitress? It's her second or third day I think."

Chris turned and looked at his waitress, "Uh, no. No. That's alright. I'm sure I'll meet her."

The waitress laughed, "It's okay Chris. She's really sweet. Give me a sec."

As the waitress walked over to Angel, Chris watched and then became conscious of the fact that he was watching. He turned his head quick and looked back at his sketchpad, trying to keep himself from being conspicuous.

The waitress whispered in Angel's ear and Angel nodded. Then, she looked over at the man sitting at the table. The light coming through the window behind him turned his face dark. But, it was unmistakable. That was the man in her sketches. She instantly connected with him and had no idea why.

Chris felt a tingling that started in the back of his head and then made his neck burn. He turned to look at her and they were locked in a stare. Neither knew what to do nor what to say. But, neither could turn away.

Chapter XX

Chris started coming into the diner every day Kissy worked. He would look for her section and when she saw him, she would point to it. Putting her hands on her hips and cocking her leg with a cute smile, she would nod her head and that's where he would sit.

The other waitresses would come over and say hello, but they knew he had chosen his favorite. That's just the way it was going to be. Once in a while he would bring a gift for one of the other waitresses if it was her birthday or there was some other reason. But, everyone knew that Kissy's section was where he would sit.

He made it a point to come in close to the end of her shift. She would grab him a cup of coffee and then wait on him until her shift was over. Then, she would sit down with him and they would talk. They couldn't describe it themselves, but there was a connection that kept building and building over time.

Chris had entertained the thought that she could be a part of his life somehow, in the life before his coma. But, that thought was quickly dismissed when Kissy talked so lively about her father. Chris did ask if it was possible that he could meet him. But, Kissy's eyes grew sad as she looked back at Chris. It was almost as if she was looking through him.

"The reason I'm working here is because he passed away," Kissy explained.

"Oh, I'm sorry to hear that," Chris felt a touch of grief for a man he had never met.

Kissy went off into thought, and then she lifted her head, "No. No. Mom said it was bound to happen one day anyway."

"What do you mean," Chris asked.

"Well, he was always doing things. Things that could, or should have killed him a million times," Kissy let out a soft laugh. She shook her head.

Chris studied her hard, "You don't have to tell me…"

"Oh um, no," Kissy answered. "Not at all." Kissy paused and then continued, "Well, when they bought me the car they told me that I had to get a job. They couldn't afford to pay the insurance. I mean, my dad was an animal catcher and all. But you know, we just didn't have everything we wanted. We had everything we needed. Just not everything we wanted and I needed to get a job to help."

"So, you started here," Chris asked.

"Actually, no," Kissy answered with a laugh. "Actually, my dad came to me and asked if I would mind running some moonshine for him. He would pay me enough to cover the insurance and some extra money for myself. Now, mom didn't know about that. She told him he had to give up the moonshine when he got the job as the animal catcher. But, he didn't do that. People had come to rely on him and it was hard for him to walk away. But, I had to hide it from mom and dad didn't make that easy. He would ask me right in front of her. One time, I had to get her a fancy dress because she was asking questions. So, I played it off like it was a surprise for her."

Chris was shocked, "You ran moonshine?"

"Oh, it was fine," Kissy waved her hand. "I knew everyone. I grew up knowing them all."

"Yeah but, you were running moonshine," Chris was still shocked.

Kissy looked at Chris having no idea what point he was trying to make, "Yeah, I was running moonshine."

"Wow! I'm speechless," Chris said.

"Why," Kissy responded.

"You were sixteen and you were running moonshine," Chris answered.

"Oh," Kissy finally picked up what Chris meant. "No, like I said, I knew all the people I was delivering to, had known them all my life. Anyway, he made the moonshine in the barn. Mom never went out there. She was afraid of what she might find because he was always doing something."

"Like what," Chris asked.

"Oh, I don't know, like he made bombs and he was always trying to invent stuff," Kissy answered. "And that's why mom said it was bound to happen. She always knew he was going to die long before he got a chance to grow old."

"So, he pretty much did whatever he wanted out in the barn," Chris asked.

"Yeah, mom never went out there until that one time. She got the weirdest feeling and she went out to check on him.

I went with her because when mom got a feeling like that, she was normally right and I wanted to know myself."

"What happened," Chris asked.

"Mom always said that he would blow himself up, but that never happened. Then, when he got the job as an animal catcher, she was sure something was going to get a hold of him one day. I mean, he was going up against some really nasty critters. But, that's not what happened either. It's funny though that it did not surprise mom one bit. Well, it hurt. I mean, she lost the love of her life that day. She didn't deal with it very well for quite some time. In fact, that's why I'm working now. I have to help out or she'll just fall apart. Anyway, he liked to make his moonshine and sell it. But, he liked to taste it first. One day, we found him in the shed. He had knocked over everything and was just lying there on the floor, white as a ghost."

"Moonshine killed him?"

"Oh no! No, not at all. He could drink his share of moonshine. Mom and the doctor both say he got a hold of something else."

"Like what?"

"Well, I don't know for sure. But, he had different concoctions all over the place that he could have mistaken for his moonshine. There was bleach, mold cleaner, it's hard to say. Who knows?"

"He mistook it for his moonshine? How do you mistake bleach for moonshine," Chris asked.

"Ever had any?"

"No!"

"Yeah, it can make you loopy. It made him real loopy. Mom says he drank more than his share of it. So, the doctor says he must have reached for his moonshine and wasn't paying attention to what he was grabbing. It didn't take long to kill him. They said it was a pretty violent death the way everything was knocked over and stuff was spilled all over the place."

"That is so sad," Chris empathized. "So, are you guys doing alright now?"

"Yeah, actually," Kissy answered. "I didn't know how easy it was for us. We only have like a few bills, nothing much. The house is ours. Been in the family for years. So, I'm actually able to do it myself. Mom doesn't have to work, and that's a good thing too because she just isn't the same anymore."

"I can imagine," Chris thought.

"Um, she told me to tell you thanks by the way," Kissy said.

"For what," Chris asked.

"Well when she found out you came in the diner, she told me to tell you thanks for giving her one of your paintings," Kissy announced.

Chris thought about it for a moment and then he remembered, "Oh, that was her! That's right. You were there. I remember that now. Well, tell her I said she's welcome."

As Chris remembered that moment, so did Kissy. She studied Chris's face and thought about the silhouette. But, she had no idea what to think. It was just some strange coincidence that he looked like the guy who haunted her dreams while she was struggling with a fever.

Chapter XXI

Kissy sat down in a huff. Chris looked up from his sketch to see why she was upset. She looked at the sketch and pulled it to her, "Your sketching!"

"Yeah," Chris responded. "I sketch before I paint."

"No, not that," Kissy continued. "It looks like how I sketch."

"Really," Chris perked up with interest.

"Yeah, I've only been doing it for a little while, maybe a few years. But yeah, I sketch."

"What do you sketch," Chris asked.

When Kissy thought about it, she quickly realized that she had said enough. She didn't want to tell Chris about the silhouette, a vision she saw when she was sick with a fever and was never able to forget. She definitely didn't want to tell Chris how much he resembled the guy in her head, "Oh uh, I draw just different portraits and stuff. Nothing major, not anything on your level anyway. This is really good!"

Chris nodded his head, "Thank you."

"Oh, yeah sure," Kissy said with a serious look on her face.

"So, what happened," Chris asked.

"What do you mean," Kissy responded.

"When you sat down, you seemed troubled about something," Chris said.

"Oh yeah," Kissy remembered. "You would not believe what I just found out."

"What?"

"The home schooling I've been doing all my life wasn't legit," Kissy announced.

"You have got to be kidding me," Chris said shocked.

"Yeah, my mom didn't know what she was doing and didn't sign me up to a legitimate home schooling program," Kissy continued.

"That's unbelievable," Chris was still shocked. "What are you going to do?"

"Well, at the board they told me that I could take a GED test. So, I'm going to look into that," Kissy answered.

Chris nodded his head, "Actually, that's not a bad idea. You get your high school equivalent and you move on with your life."

"Yeah, I know," Kissy thought as she dropped her head. "The thing is that I should be graduating high school and walking down an aisle to get my diploma. I don't know why she didn't just do that. She home schooled me and didn't even get it right."

"I know. It is a little heartbreaking," Chris consulted. "But, look at it this way. High school is but a speck on the timeline of life. It's such a small part and then you move on. After college, it won't matter anyway."

"College," Kissy asked. "I don't think I'm college material."

"You would be surprised. I think you have more potential than you give yourself credit," Chris urged.

"Really," Kissy asked. "You think I should go to college? Did you go to college?"

Chris thought about that for a moment, "I don't know."

"Oh, I'm sorry," Kissy felt awful. By now, she knew the story, "I didn't mean to…"

"No, it's fine," Chris said. "It's actually kind of interesting. There's this whole other life I know nothing about.

I think about it every once in a while and I get to imagine different things. Like, I was a teacher or a soldier in a whole other life. But, I have no idea."

Kissy just shook her head. Kissy thought how sad it all was. Chris had no idea what his whole life had been. What if he *was* a teacher or a highly decorated soldier? He had no idea who he actually was and that was something that hit Kissy pretty hard.

Chris stood at the door of his secret room, looking over the paintings he had painted of the one he used to call Angel. The last painting he had completed of her was of her standing in front of the house across the street. But recently, he had stopped painting her. There were no visits. There were no inspirations.

As Chris admired his paintings, he thought of Kissy. It was such a tragedy that her mother had no idea what she was doing when it came to her daughter's education. Why didn't she just let the poor girl go to school? She should be able to enjoy the things in life that all the other kids take for granted.

But, Chris also entertained another thought. For not being properly educated, Kissy had turned out just fine. Chris didn't have much experience with people, but Kissy was certainly more intelligent than most. Chris concluded that intelligence is something that can't be taught. A person either has it or they don't.

Somehow, Kissy had been given a great mind by a guy who mistook bleach for moonshine and a lady who bungled her daughter's education. Chris didn't find it funny, but he couldn't help but chuckle at the thought of those two. How in the world had they raised that girl without accidently blowing her up or getting her stabbed in a back alley running moonshine? He just shook his head as all these thoughts hit him pretty hard.

That's when she startled him. She had been standing behind him for about a minute. The look on Amy's face was priceless. She had been rendered speechless by what she was seeing. Then, she finally spoke, "They are beautiful!"

Chris's heart jumped. Then, it started beating fast. Worlds just collided. The secret was revealed. Chris turned to look at Amy who was still stunned.

"I thought you said that you couldn't do portraits," Amy said.

"I told you that," Chris answered. "Yes, I might have said something to that effect."

"These are wonderful," Amy admired. "I don't understand. Why wouldn't you tell me about these?"

Chris stared at Amy for a moment, thinking of what he could possibly say. But, nothing came to him. He had to just fess up and tell Amy the truth, "I have been painting this girl for years. I get different visions of her that I can't shake and I have to paint her. I think she is in some way connected to my past."

"But, why keep it a secret," Amy asked.

"I didn't want to let her go," Chris answered. "She's not something I wanted to sell."

"I would have understood that," Amy responded. Then, she thought, "That girl at the restaurant. Is it her?"

"No. I've been painting these long before I met her," Chris answered.

"They look just like her," Amy mentioned.

"I know," Chris said as he moved to the kitchen. "The thing is I haven't painted her since I met Kissy."

Amy followed Chris to the kitchen, "Well, let's do something with them. I don't have to sell them. But, we can show them."

"Show them," Chris asked.

"Yeah, we'll do a showing," Amy repeated. "After, you can bring them home and put them back in the room."

"I don't know," Chris responded. "I'll think about it."

"Well, think about it hard," Amy urged. "These are good and people will love to see them."

Chapter XXII

Chris watched as Kissy laughed hardily. There were times when she was unhappy talking about the passing of her father. But most of the time, she recalled her life with Gilmer as one big ride with lots of wild turns and always a good time, if not hysterical in the least. It could make anyone laugh.

Apparently, when Gilmer had been given the job as an animal catcher, he was told that he would be using bombs. So, he went to work every day waiting patiently for his chance to blow up something. He came home every evening with the same story that he didn't get to blow anything up that day, but he knew it was coming soon. They kept promising him that one day he would get to use a bomb.

Maggie got tired of repeating herself, "They are pulling your leg Gil. They don't blow up porches and stuff like that."

But, Gilmer insisted and he kept going to work with the hope that one day he would get to use a bomb. Then, he came into the house one evening and he didn't have anything to say about bombing. In fact, he was very quiet and it wasn't like him.

So, Krista asked, "Dad, what's wrong?"

"Oh, nothing honey," Gilmer answered.

But, Maggie had picked up on his different attitude too, "What happened today Gil?"

"It's no big deal," Gilmer answered again.

"Come on," Maggie insisted. "You aren't acting right. Something must have happened."

Gilmer had his hands in his pockets as he looked around at both of the ladies in the living room, "Well ok, I got to use a bomb today."

"What? They actually blow stuff up," Maggie was shocked.

Krista's eyes were big too, "Well that's great daddy!"

"No, not really," Gilmer finally mentioned after a moment. "They're not real bombs."

Maggie slapped her hand towel on her arm, "I told you Gil."

Maggie was laughing as Gilmer looked at her seriously, "Alright now, you were right."

"Well, what were they," Krista asked.

"They are smoke bombs and they're for pests," Gilmer answered. "The family leaves the house for a few hours and we bomb their house with smoke."

"Oh, those things," Krista realized.

"Yeah, those things," Gilmer agreed.

"Well, I could have told you that," Krista mentioned.

"Well, I wish you would have," Gilmer thought.

As Kissy told the story with a hearty laugh, Chris chuckled, "So, he actually thought he was going to blow up someone's house or barn?"

"Who knows what was going on in his mind," Kissy shook her head. "But, you should have seen his face. It was so pitiful. I felt bad for him, but mom went on about knowing animal catchers don't blow up porches."

"That Gilmer," Chris shook his head. "I don't know what to think about him."

"What do you mean," Kissy asked.

"Oh no," Chris started to answer. "I don't mean anything by it at all. I'm just saying he was quite a guy."

"Oh, you can say it," Kissy confirmed. "He was quite the character. I don't mind!"

Chris laughed and Kissy laughed right along with him. As she giggled and looked out the window, Kissy's smile was so contagious. Chris couldn't help but smile with her. He studied her for a moment.

In his mind, he had stopped debating whether or not to have the showing. It was good for him. It was good for Amy. He was going to do it. But, he was now debating whether or not to invite Kissy. They had grown so close. Would she understand? He didn't know whether or not to take that chance.

Amy could just feel that Chris would be in the kitchen as she barged into the front door. She walked in with a huge smile on her face expecting an answer. She stood in the middle of the living room with her hands on her hips and waited patiently.

Chris looked up from his paper and took a drink of his coffee. He eyed her for a moment as if he had no idea what she wanted. But, he knew. He liked joking with her, "What uh, what can I do for you today?"

"Chris, tell me!"

"I'm sorry, what do you want to know," Chris asked.

"Are you going to do the showing or not," Amy stamped her foot knowing full well that Chris was joking around with her, and that was a good thing.

"Of course, I'm doing it," Chris answered. "Have I ever said no to you?"

Amy was excited! She threw her hands up in the air like she was celebrating just winning a race. Then, she strolled into the kitchen, "That's great! I'm so glad because I have a secret for you."

"What's that?"

Amy looked at Chris with a deep stare and a huge smile on her face, "I already have everything in place. It's going to be shown in the Cultural Center next month, and I have a truck coming in a week to get the collection."

Chris looked at her and cocked his head, "Whoa! That's so soon!"

"Too soon," Amy asked suddenly concerned that maybe she was pushing a little too much.

Chris thought for a moment, "No, I guess it's like ripping off a scab, the faster the better."

Amy pounded on the kitchen bar, "That's the spirit!"

Chris looked at Amy knowing he had made a good decision, but double-guessing himself. It was just a showing of his art. In fact if he knew anything about Amy, all he had to do was show up and look good. She would take care of everything else for him.

As Chris walked around his house thinking of everything, he ventured into Angel's room. He saw the dollhouse in the middle of the room with nothing else around it. Why had he only made that one thing for Angel? But, there were many unanswered questions.

Why had he stopped painting Angel? Then, he remembered how much pain that used to bring him. Not when she visited, but when she faded away. He would feel a greater sense of loneliness than he ever had, and that was the hard part. But, he hadn't felt that in a long while. When did it go away? Why hadn't he noticed until now?

He was still standing at Angel's door having all of these thoughts, but he was staring at the floor. As he looked at the dollhouse again, he could remember Angel admiring it. Then, another memory hit him.

We have our memories.

Try to remember me.

Close your eyes and I'll be there.

Think about me

And I will think about you.

In our minds we'll be together.

The times we spend apart

We'll be together.

That's all you have to do when you miss me.

"There was that song again," Chris thought as he heard it in the voice of Angel he had created with his imagination. But, the memories he had of his Angel were fading and Chris had no idea why. Was it years of dealing with loneliness and loss when he finally learned to cope? Had he got to the point where he no longer needed her as a coping mechanism?

Chris started down the stairs still in deep thought. As he thought of the years that he had cultivated a relationship with someone who wasn't real, he made it to the bottom of the steps where he looked in on his secret paintings that were no longer a secret. They were about to be revealed to the world and what was harder for him to think about, they were about ready to be revealed to Kissy who looked so much like them.

Standing there at the door admiring the last painting of her that he had painted, he remembered that day so vividly. That's when she became real to him. The girl at the river and the girl in front of the house seemed to be his Angel in real life.

Could that be it? Could Kissy have replaced his need to fill his life with someone imaginary? It didn't make sense. Chris talked to Amy, who had become a great friend of his over the years. Chris had made quite a few other friends.

One question lingered in the air because Chris was afraid to ask it. He was afraid to think it. He finally decided it didn't matter. Chris had learned a long time ago never to question the paths he was given to cross. To wonder what was so special about a certain person, what was so different about them, was not his to judge.

Chapter XXIII

Chris found himself in a pretty tough situation. He really wanted to invite Kissy to the showing. But, he didn't want her to see the paintings he had been painting of a person he had referred to as Angel for as long as he could remember.

It wasn't the only thoughts he had entertained throughout the day. But, whether or not to invite Kissy dominated his thoughts between conversations about the invitees, decorations and displays. Amy had mentioned putting together the Hidden Room because she was inspired by the fact that he had kept the room secret for so many years.

Chris thought the Hidden Room was a great idea! It became an even better idea when he heard Amy say that the room would be in the back behind all the partitions displaying his other art. But, Amy clarified that being hidden was just an illusion. Of course, it wouldn't be hidden. That was too much for Chris to ask.

Amy was running around and making everything happen. Just as Chris thought, all he had to do was sit back and approve certain decisions. But, what decisions were there really to make? What champagne to serve? How to accommodate all the parking?

Often, it felt to Chris like he was a fifth wheel on a wagon and it was his own art event. But, it gave him more time to visit Kissy at the diner. After all, Amy was just down the street if she needed him. They were focused on the showing and there was very little art for him to produce at this point. His furniture was being mass-produced by some manufacturer a couple hundred miles away. The diner was where he belonged.

While Kissy was serving him, she seemed very excited to share something. So Chris waited patiently for her break, which felt like it was taking longer and longer with every new person who entered the diner and chose her section. Chris drank refill after refill of coffee until he felt like he was going to overdose on caffeine.

But, Kissy's break finally came. She sat down with a smile on her face. But, she sighed and rolled her eyes first. It had been a long day and it was going to be even longer day. Kissy had started her day off with one thing to tell Chris, but now she had two.

"So, guess what," she started.

"What?"

"I took the GED," Kissy said with a smile.

Chris nodded his head. But, that conversation had taken place months ago. Plus, the smile on Kissy's face was his final clue, "And you passed?"

"Well," Kissy hesitated.

Chris's eyebrows were raised in surprise. His mouth registered a partial smile while it was wide open patiently waiting to hear the rest of what Kissy had to say.

"Of course I passed," Kissy continued. "You ruined my surprise. How did you know?"

"You wouldn't have been so excited all day to tell me if you failed," Chris answered.

"Hmm, that makes sense," Kissy thought. "So, guess what I'm going to do!"

Chris studied her expression long and hard, "Ok, I have no read on this one."

"Good! I have a surprise left," Kissy joked. "I'm going to register into the community college."

Chris's eyes were wide. He nodded for a moment and then he lifted his hands to softly clap at the table, "That's what I'm talking about."

"Oh stop," Kissy said as if blushing. Then jokingly, "No really, stop it!"

Chris shared a short chuckle, "No actually, that's good news."

"Thank you," Kissy smiled as she looked deep into Chris's eyes.

He was still debating whether or not to invite her to the showing. His heart was pulling him toward asking her to attend. But, his mind was pulling him away.

The debate going on in Chris's head was shattered when he heard Kissy say, "So, I'm buying a new dress for your art thing. That's the second thing I've been dying to tell you."

Chris was immediate to react with a smile. But, his heart was pounding nearly out of his chest. He had no control over whether or not he could keep her from it. Then he was informed that multiple worlds of his had finally collided. Deep layers of his soul were about to be revealed.

"That Amy is a really nice lady," Kissy continued. "She said she tracked me down in here just to let me know that she would love me to come to your art event."

"Well, that was great of her," Chris said as his mind was racing a million miles an hour. "I'm glad she did that."

"I am too," Kissy agreed. "I finally get to do something cultural, something more than the day in and day out. I'm going to be a college girl soon and I should have more of that in my life. Don't you think?"

"Absolutely," Chris nodded, "Without a doubt!"

Chris adjusted his tie and grabbed another glass of champagne as the server passed. Suits were not his thing. But, he looked like a million bucks. Amy had told him a hundred times and he was starting to get the idea.

As he stood in the middle of the room, he waited anxiously for Kissy to make her appearance. Looking every time the door opened, Chris became more anxious with each new person who walked in the doors. He greeted people and talked about his art. The conversations seemed to pass the time and distract him from what was making him the most anxious.

But, they were only quick fixes for the time. The more he wanted her to come, the longer it seemed to take. But, the time finally came. She walked through the door in the most modest dress. But, it looked great on her.

She looked around the room and spotted him right away. He was hard to miss, the guy in a tux standing in the middle of the room. She did a little curtsy when she saw him and then she walked the long distance across the expansive room with partitions that drew attention to the center.

"Hey you, you look great," Chris complimented Kissy as she approached him.

"Yeah, you're not so bad yourself," Kissy returned.

By then Amy had joined them, "Hey Kissy, so glad you could make it!"

Kissy beamed, "I wouldn't have missed it for nothing."

Amy waved over a server and handed Kissy a glass. Chris shook his head and tapped Amy on her hip, "She's not twenty-one."

"That's fine," Amy insisted. "It's non-alcoholic."

"I've been drinking non-alcoholic champagne," Chris asked.

"Oh no," Amy answered. "I made sure you had the good stuff. I thought you could use it."

"You got non-alcohol champagne just for me," Kissy asked.

Amy laughed, "Actually, it's for quite a few of our guests. Mr. Ferlin here has quite a following with the younger art admirers."

"Really," Kissy asked.

"Oh yes," Amy confirmed. "They're part of the Insider's Secret fad."

"Insider's Secret," Kissy felt a hint of mystery.

"Oh yeah," Amy continued. "It started when an article about him featured in Line and Edge, which is an influential art magazine. The college students from the School of Arts were immediately taken in by the fact that he is the buzz among the rich and the famous. Of course when the art college kids like something, the high school college kids are in. Throughout the night, plenty of underage admirers have been coming and going."

"Wow," Kissy looked at Chris impressed.

"Come on," Amy urged. "Let me show you around."

"That would be great," Kissy said.

As the two walked off together, Chris thought he'd just stay back. Amy was doing such a good job at breaking the ice and carrying the conversation. Not that Chris needed help talking to Kissy. But, he was unsure of how she was going to react to the Hidden Room.

That's when his mind turned. He wanted to see her expression. He wanted to be there when she saw the paintings for the first time and she had questions. So, he started toward the Hidden Room when he suddenly saw Kissy running across the floor toward the doors. She ran out so fast, Chris had no time to react.

His initial thought was to go after her. But then, he realized she was running away from his paintings. He was probably the last person on earth she wanted to see. Amy came around the partition and looked straight at Chris.

She shrugged her shoulders and mouthed the words, "I'm sorry!"

Chris had no idea what to say as he looked at Amy and then toward the doors that were still closing.

Chapter XXIV

Amy sat silently at Chris's kitchen bar with a look of deep concern on her face. She had just stopped in to see how he was doing. With a freshly poured cup of coffee and a slightly guilty conscience, Amy offered Chris her undivided attention.

"I don't get it," Chris shook his head. "She hasn't been in the diner for a few days."

"Have you asked," Amy wondered.

"No," Chris answered. "I didn't want to look like I was trying to be a pest."

Amy nodded her head. She could understand completely. Chris already felt as if in some way, he had violated the little girl's privacy. It was strange how Chris thought. But, Amy had chalked it up a long time ago as being one of his quirks.

Chris was the type of person to give someone their space. He didn't feel comfortable smothering anyone. He got absolutely nothing out of asking anyone for their approval. And Chris hadn't figured out what he and Kissy were even about, as far as her life was concerned. He certainly didn't feel right demanding his place in it.

"I think it will be alright if you go into town and ask about her," Amy finally urged. In her way of thinking, that's what normal people do. Chris needed to hear that it was fine to do what normal people would do.

Chris shook his head and then took a drink of his coffee, "I mean I want to. That's what I want to do."

"Then go," Amy pushed again. "Everyone knows you have a friendship. It's ok to ask."

Chris looked at Amy, "You think?"

"Yes," Amy answered. "I wouldn't say it if I didn't mean it!"

Chris cocked his head as he stared at Amy. Those were words he understood. Don't say them if you don't mean them. With that Chris pounded on the table, "Ok then, I'll go into town and demand her whereabouts. We need to talk this one through."

Amy raised her eyebrow at the new charge that had just overtaken Chris, "Can I finish my coffee first?"

"Oh sure, absolutely!"

One of the waitresses noticed Chris as soon as he walked in the door. She waved him to her section and then looked around behind the counter before walking over to Chris and offering him some coffee.

"Sure, uh yes I'll have a cup," Chris answered. "Have you seen Kissy?"

"Actually," the waitress answered, "She was in here yesterday looking for you. You must have just missed each other. Anyway, she left this for you. I'll go get your coffee."

The look on the waitress's face was very telling. She was sad and simply nodded at the folder she had placed on the table in front of him. It had a note on it, "Please give to Mr. Ferlin."

As Chris watched the waitress walk away, he felt a strange churning in the pit of his stomach. Looking down at the folder in front of him, he wondered what it could possibly be. But, he hesitated. He wasn't too sure he was going to like what was inside.

Slowly, he untied the binder and opened the flap. The waitress poured him a cup of coffee and then gave him his privacy. She walked away as he pulled out a pile of sketches with a note on top.

Dear Mr. Ferlin,

    I'm so sorry for running out of your art exhibit the other night. That was not the best way to handle that and I'm sure you would like an explanation.

    The fact is that when I saw those paintings, I saw myself. I didn't know what to think at first. That's because I have been drawing sketches and they remind me so much of you.

    Then after my father died, I guess I just needed someone to take his place and you were there. I've never felt so alone because mom hasn't been the same. She keeps to herself and I don't feel like she's even here anymore.

Anyway, I wrote a poem and I wanted to share it with you. The sketches I've been drawing are in here too. I promise to stay in touch.

Love,

Kissy

Chris looked at the poem and then he put it to the side as he stared at the top sketch. It was a drawing of him sitting in a booth at the diner. There was a very remarkable likeness, which he had learned himself is difficult to achieve in art sometimes.

He noticed his own drawing techniques. Scribbles and hard lines seemed to jump around from point to point. They shared the same style. Then, he recalled her making that point when she saw his sketches for the first time.

The next drawing caught him by surprise. It was a fairly good resemblance of him standing across the street. Chris couldn't help but think how bizarre the coincidences were. No wonder Kissy ran out of the Cultural Center the way she did. He had painted her and she had sketched him of the same moment when they saw each other on the street.

His mind began to really race when he saw the next sketch. It was of him painting on the river. What was going on? Why was she sketching him and why was he painting her? There was something unexplainable happening. But, Chris started to truly understand why Kissy was pulling herself away from him.

The next ten to fifteen sketches were of a dark man with an umbrella. Chris had no idea what those drawings were. He could see the resemblance, but he couldn't make the connection.

He looked over at the poem. Then, he picked it up and began reading it. He didn't fully understand it at first but then the meaning hit him.

My Broken Piano

Bing, out of tune

Bing, bing, a clash out of tune

But, sweet to my ears

Burned dolls on the floor

Dirty blankets with holes

An old ripped coloring book

And a broken piano

What do I remember first?

There's so much and it's not all there

Before my memories fade

Grab it all in and don't let it go!

It's a part of you

It makes the you

The who no one knows

They never know

Just you and your broken piano

Pieces of you all over the floor

You want what? There isn't any more

You didn't have the life others had

They were getting ahead, and you…

You were playing that damn broken piano

You were stuck with that damn broken piano

Dragging it everywhere you go

Won't even leave it behind once

Won't let it alone for a minute

It felt like betraying an old friend

If you closed it up and walked away

Because it was there too

Through everything about you

Years later, you've grown

It's still there in your room

Wrap your arms around yourself

And remember the you

The who no one ever knew

No one will ever know

It's always just me and my broken piano

As he finished reading the poem, he saw the waitress standing above him, "She's gone! I've lost her!"

The waitress shook her head, "No, Mr. Ferlin. She still works here. She's just taking a few days off because her mother passed away."

Chapter XXV

Early in the morning, the ground was still wet from the heavy rain. But it had let up to a dull grey aura, perfect air for a funeral. Chris saw Kissy, a lonely mourner standing by the casket as the minister read scripture and talked about life after death.

Amy had accompanied Chris as they stood in the distance, observing from the hill. Chris felt like he had no reason being there, but Amy had encouraged him to go. They knew very little about Kissy. But, they knew enough to know that Kissy would most likely be the only one to attend her mom's funeral.

Kissy looked up at the two lone people standing on the hill as she dried her eyes with her tissue. Lonely was not the word to express how she felt. Helpless was less than suitable to describe how lost she was, and how big the world now seemed to her.

She did manage a slight smile when she saw Chris in the distance. The short exchange drew him closer to her as he began to walk down the hill and join her by her side. They stood quietly as the minister ended his service.

"Earth to earth, ashes to ashes, dust to dust..." the minister spoke as he threw dirt on the casket and it was lowered into the grave.

Kissy approached the casket and dropped a rose into the grave. Then she stepped backward to join Chris. His heart was heavy, but he didn't have any words to say. Kissy wasn't looking for any words of consoling. She just enjoyed having his company.

They watched as the casket steadily lowered out of sight. The minister shook Kissy's hand and said a few words of encouragement. Then, he walked away and left Chris and Kissy to their own grieving.

Kissy turned to Chris, "Thank you for coming."

Chris turned and looked at her, still not knowing fully what to say, "I wasn't sure. But, I'm glad I did."

He took her hand and led her away from her mom's grave. They walked up the hill toward Amy when the rain started to fall again. Kissy had been playing with something around her neck.

When Chris opened his umbrella, he turned to cover her and saw the locket she had kept all these years. He looked harder at the locket and then reached up to touch it. When she looked up at him, she saw the silhouette with the umbrella.

"Kissy, it's bootiful," Chris uttered.

A little girl flashed before his eyes. He could see her at the stove helping him make pancakes. He could see her at the river, sitting in his lap.

"It's bootiful daddy," Kissy repeated. She could see the man who left the apartment. She could see him on the couch as they watched a movie. She could see him at the jewelry store giving her the locket.

Staring in each other's eyes, they knew what no words could express. Tears rolled down Kissy's face, "What is happening? What is going on?"

"Your name is Krista, Krista Ferlin. And you are my daughter," Chris answered.

"Why? How could this be?"

"It's a long story. But, I lost you years ago. You have been my little Angel."

"All you are to me is a dark silhouette with an umbrella."

"That's the last time you saw me. That's the last time I held you in my arms, and I went away that night," tears started rolling down Chris's cheek.

"This is so confusing," Kissy said as she shook her head.

"Yeah, it's true," Chris said. "We have so much to talk about and catch up on. But, everything's going to be alright. I've got my little Kissy back, and now I remember you."

THE END

The Poetry of *A River in the Ocean*

When You Miss Me

We have our memories.

Try to remember me.

Close your eyes and I'll be there.

Think about me

And I will think about you.

In our minds we'll be together.

The times we spend apart

We'll be together.

That's all you have to do when you miss me.

In Memory of an Angel

I remember. I remember you!

On a warm day…

On the porch swing in the sunlight.

With your flowers…

Singing church songs in your white dress.

I was standing by you when you fell down

And took your last breath.

You were not so old then…

They played the violin over your coffin.

Angel! I want to know where do the angels go.

I want to know who hides the Sun.

I want to know who keeps watch of you

All through the night.

Angel! Tell the angels you have come.

Tell them I already have one!

A hundred years ago…I've grown a few since
Then.

A thousand miles…a million people I have met.

And yet I still come home to find the place

Where you were laid.

In all my travels…

It's not any easier to get through the day.

I want to know where do the angels go.

I want to know who hides the sun.

I want to know who keeps watch of you

All through the night.

Angel! Tell the angels you have come.

Tell them I already have one!

I was just a kid.

How could you have mattered so much?

You know what they say about angels…

It only takes one touch…

I want to know where do the angels go.

I want to know who hides the sun.

I want to know who keeps watch of you

All through the night.

Angel! Tell the angels you have come.

Tell them I already have one!

My Broken Piano

Bing, out of tune

Bing, bing, a clash out of tune

But, sweet to my ears

Burned dolls on the floor

Dirty blankets with holes

An old ripped coloring book

And a broken piano

What do I remember first?

There's so much and it's not all there

Before my memories fade

Grab it all in and don't let it go!

It's a part of you

It makes the you

The who no one knows

They never know

Just you and your broken piano

Pieces of you all over the floor

You want what? There isn't any more

You didn't have the life others had

They were getting ahead, and you…

You were playing that damn broken piano

You were stuck with that damn broken piano

Dragging it everywhere you go

Won't even leave it behind once

Won't let it alone for a minute

It felt like betraying an old friend

If you closed it up and walked away

Because it was there too

Through everything about you

Years later, you've grown

It's still there in your room

Wrap your arms around yourself

And remember the you

The who no one ever knew

No one will ever know

It's always just me and my broken piano

Made in the USA
Lexington, KY
22 July 2013